Sound-Barriers

Pursuing Revival of Holy Worship

TIMOTHY SCOTT MAURICIO

Copyright © 2014 Timothy Scott Mauricio.

All rights reserved. No part of this book may be used or reproduced by any means, graphic, electronic, or mechanical, including photocopying, recording, taping or by any information storage retrieval system without the written permission of the publisher except in the case of brief quotations embodied in critical articles and reviews.

Scripture taken from the New King James Version®, copyright © 1982 by Thomas Nelson, Inc. Used by permission. All rights reserved.

Scripture quotations marked (ESV) are from The ESV® Bible (The Holy Bible, English Standard Version®) copyright © 2001 by Crossway, a publishing company of Good News Publishers. Used by permission. All rights reserved.

Scripture quotations marked NLT are taken from the Holy Bible, New Living Translation, copyright © 1996, 2004, 2007 by Tyndale House Foundation. Used by permission of Tyndale House Publishers Inc. Carol Stream, Illinois 60188. All rights reserved.

Scriptures taken from the Holy Bible, *New International Version*® *NIV*®, Copyright © 1973, 1978, 1984 by Biblica, Inc.™ Used by permission of Zondervan. All rights reserved worldwide.

Dedication

To my family:

To Monica: My loving wife, confidant, and constant encourager of thirty years. Words will never be able to convey the depth of love and thankfulness I have for you. Your commitment and steadfast devotion to God, our family, and myself exemplifies what it means to be a godly woman!

To my daughter, Brittney; my son, Dallas; and his wife, Kaydee: Thank you for always speaking the truth, for never holding back your insights or feelings, and most importantly for your support, encouragement, humor, and love!

Contents

Foreword xi
Acknowledgments xv

Section 1   An Overture to the Pursuit of Holy Worship 1

    Chapter 1   Read This First! 3
    Chapter 2   A Prelude to Worship 6
    Chapter 3   Resounding Impact 8
    Chapter 4   An Awakening to Revival of Holy Worship 12

Section 2   The Prominent Barriers Obstructing Holy
              Worship 17

    Chapter 5   The Barrier of Unholy Irreverence 19
    Chapter 6   The Entrapment of Entertainment 26
    Chapter 7   The Obstruction of Production 30
    Chapter 8   The Impediment of Me 32
    Chapter 9   The By-Product Protrusion 35
    Chapter 10   The Checkpoint of Consumerism 39
    Chapter 11   The Cost Deterrent of Worship 42
    Chapter 12   The Musical Mandate Roadblock 45
    Chapter 13   The Barricade of Comparison 52

Chapter 14	Encumbered by Pride and Ego	56
Chapter 15	Who's In Charge? A Snag in Supremacy!	64
Chapter 16	The Discipleship Drawback	70
Chapter 17	Preventing Presence While Promoting Programs	77
Chapter 18	The Blockade of Busyness	81
Chapter 19	Compromising: A Detour from Commitment	84
Section 3	A Journey Beyond the Barriers	89
Chapter 20	A Shift Toward Worshipping in Spirit and Truth	91
Chapter 21	Returning to Christ	96
Chapter 22	Beneath the Cross of Christ Jesus	100
Chapter 23	Christ's Positional Preeminence	104
Chapter 24	No Sidestepping Sin or Moving from Grace	107
Chapter 25	The Far Side of Lyrics	112
Chapter 26	Beyond Our Culture of Chaos	119
Chapter 27	Heading to the Harvest—Sow What?	123
Chapter 28	From Repression To Revival	128
Chapter 29	Before John 3:16	131
Chapter 30	Forward in Prayer: A Progression of Worship	136
Chapter 31	The Journey of Obedience: Evidence of Worship	140
Chapter 32	Crossing from Commitment to Feelings	144

Section 4   Inspiration Toward Holy Worship 149

    Chapter 33 Seven Indispensible Truths of
                            Acceptable Worship 151

    Chapter 34 Seven Reverent Postures of a
                            Worshipful Heart 155

    Chapter 35 A Biblical Consideration of God's
                            Perfect Attributes 160

    Chapter 36 God's Attributes:
                            A Concise Biblical Study 163

Prayerful Closing 177
Timothy's Mission 179

Foreword

Tim Mauricio has gracefully endured more significant life-altering changes than anyone I know. The first time I met Tim, he embraced me as if I had been a longtime friend. His ability to connect with people and engage them on a very sincere level is a gift from the Spirit. It was clear to me that people were naturally drawn to Tim, who was (and continues to be) a compassionate leader. Tim demonstrates, on a consistent basis, servant leadership.

His love of music was apparent, even to a musically challenged person like me. He not only played music, he wrote and composed music and had an ear for all things harmonic. Worship music was his passion.

Then his life changed. He was robbed of his most precious sense: sound. Due to the growing and complex tumors in his brain and ensuing surgeries to save the longevity of his life, it cost him his most valued earthly gift. He no longer hears music. He no longer can sense the timbre in one's voice.

The impact of such an event naturally results in a continued and prolonged level of grief. Tim was no different in this regard. However, his ability to overcome the ongoing pain and grief has been nothing less than amazing. I have been able to personally experience and view his progress and attitude during the past several years. Tim has persisted in his walk with Christ and has built a strong testimony that continues to impact those around him.

Although Tim is now deaf, which is considered by most a handicap, I believe that this "handicap" has enhanced his other senses *and*, most importantly, his attention to the written word. Tim takes the time to deepen his understanding of what the text is attempting to describe or explain. Specifically, he studies the sacred Word of God, the Holy Bible. This dedication to his faith, coupled with his thirst for truth in an unfair world, drove Tim to become a committed student of the Word. He is a dedicated follower of Christ first, and loving husband and father second, and a great friend to many that know him.

It has become apparent to me that I am the one "handicapped" in this relationship as it relates to understanding the Scripture with true depth. Although it is difficult for me to admit this, I do not have the level of commitment to reading, rereading, and developing a comprehension to the Word of God that Tim has established. I can physically hear the spoken word, where Tim cannot hear. Tim, on the other hand, can "hear" the message that Christ shares through the gospel's written Word.

I ask you, who is more fortunate? Who is more handicapped?

Tim is humble yet gifted in ways that I will never understand. He has written this book in an effort to impart his thoughts and perspective so that we may better respect all barriers the Enemy has created in order to hinder our ability to effectively worship. I would like to "hear" what Tim "hears" through the written Word.

For those of you longing for an enriched walk with the Father, I encourage you to read, then reread this book. It will bless and impact you in a meaningful way. Tim's goal is to communicate his insight with you, and if his effort can impact a single life, his investment in time has been worth this process.

Torrey Larsen
President, Security One Lending

Acknowledgments

To Dan Foley, my friend of nearly thirty years. Thank you for your encouragement and for challenging me to write from my heart the lessons God has been teaching me all these years. Your wisdom and truthful feedback throughout the writing of this book made it possible for it to come to fruition!

To Nikki Thirtle, my dear friend. You truly exemplify what it means to worship in spirit and truth. I'm forever grateful for having had the rich blessing of recording music with you and the experience of witnessing your heart of worship!

Special Gratitude

To Craig Caster at Family Discipleship Ministries: I am honored, humbled, and most thankful by your continued investment of speaking God's truth into my life!

To Gerry Davey at Roy Hession Book Trust: I'm very grateful for your gracious permission to quote Roy and Revel Hession and for your encouraging, supportive words for me to pursue publishing this book.

To Barbara Andreasson at *Harper's Magazine*: Thank you for your kind consideration in permitting me to quote from one of your published articles.

Section 1

AN OVERTURE TO THE PURSUIT OF HOLY WORSHIP

Chapter 1

Read This First!

Over the years, there have been several Christian ministers whom I've grown very fond of through their writings. The candor and directness in which they communicated their insights and God's Word of truth permeate the pages onto which they are written. The sermons they preached captured in text echo within my mind, as though I could have heard them speak their messages of such biblical truth, which they so passionately conveyed. The published works of such notable persons as Charles Haddon Spurgeon, Andrew Murray, Matthew Henry, Aiden W. Tozer, J. Vernon McGee, and Roy Hession, among others have become personal treasures within my library.

These men all possessed godly discernment and had incredible depth of spiritual understanding! If one were to compile all the writings, sermons, and various compilations of these men alone, I believe it would challenge the greatest biblical scholars of today to come up with any new truth from God's Word. It is only through personal testimony, observation, and revelation that I dare divulge my personal life lessons and message God has established within my heart.

> What we call wisdom is the result of all the wisdom of past ages. Our best institutions are like young trees growing upon the roots of old trunks that have crumbled away.[1]

As you read through this book, you might find a few paragraphs that may appear to be somewhat out of place within the overall context of the particular chapter. I can assure you that at times it was a little challenging for me to determine where to precisely insert the thoughts I had just written. Frequently, this dilemma would lead me toward contemplating the creating of a new chapter. Yet, I didn't want to take a biblical truth or personal experience that could be simply stated in a single paragraph or two and then feel obligated to write enough text to justify an entire chapter.

But, as I was completing the initial draft and beginning the process of prayerfully editing this book, I was struck by a most profound insight: the placement of the textual content was not nearly as important as the truth contained within it!

And so, it's with deliberate intention, I've chosen to produce a more concise format, revealing the essentials of biblical truths along with my testimony and observations. I ask you to keep that in mind as you turn the pages and seek to discover the truth within, above the location thereof.

---

1 Henry Ward Beecher (1813–1887)

My prayer, hope, and greatest desire is that your heart will be inspired, your soul blessed, and your conscience convicted as you read on.

> Fruitful and acceptable worship begins before it begins.
> —Alexander MacLaren (1826–1910)

Chapter 2

A Prelude to Worship

Having come from a musical background of intense studies and performance spanning nearly four decades, the ensuing resonating life lessons were revealed to me only after I became totally deaf. What began initially as compiling pages of my journal notes for the purpose of producing an online booklet, soon took on a new form. The result is what you have in hand!

Oftentimes, it appears to be somewhat easy for people to write with an accusatory finger, in their pointing toward others' faults and assigning blame resulting from their personal beliefs. However, that is the furthest position I want to assume in my writing this book. The mind-set I adopted while compiling my study notes and journal writings was to remain focused upon the lessons that God has been teaching me, keeping a *no holds barred* transparent and candid approach, with integrity and truthfulness in imparting my experiences. What you're about to read is my personal journey, which spans more than thirty years and includes in-depth biblical and Christian studies, experiences, conversations, observations, and most importantly, God revealing to me that which hinders holy acceptable worship unto Him.

My sincere desire as you read on is for you to examine and discover biblical truth, while being inspired to consider the barriers hindering your personal worship experiences and relationship with God.

It is with a heart of great compassion, sensitivity, and tremendous burden that I hope to communicate the significant truths God has unveiled for me to see within my own life, as well as that of many fellow Christians within the church today. As a student and minister of God's Word, I hope to communicate to you, not as one who has arrived, but as one who is on a continual journey in desiring to glorify God in all areas of my life.

Chapter 3

Resounding Impact

I often communicate to people that "I hear more now from God in my total deafness, than ever before when I had physical hearing." There is no irony to me that I've learned far greater lessons in leading others into biblical worship of God in my silence than prior to that through song. I believe it to be God's sovereign hand working in my life, whereby He allowed me to become permanently deaf. For it has had a most profound and resounding impact, allowing me to experience a much deeper relationship with Him!

Quite often, the very sense we use for one situation in life can become a distraction within that same intended purpose. Think of it like this: Have you ever begun a conversation with someone and while you were speaking, you could tell they were not listening to you? Perhaps they were listening in on someone else's dialogue ... their having eavesdropped into surrounding conversations. You know, like those types of chats where you're speaking and the other person is just totally checked out ... smiling, nodding his head to this and that as you converse with him, yet in reality, he is all but oblivious to what you're saying.

Just because someone has the capability to hear and can pass a hearing exam, doesn't mean they're always listening with the intent to hear. In the same way, there are many who have the sense of sight, yet most often are virtually blind to the life lessons being revealed about them. Such was my case, I can assure you. However, that's why I strongly believe God in His infinite wisdom and love allowed for me to become deaf ... to open the ears of my heart to hear more directly from Him!

It was during my seasons of desperation and my utmost earnest desire to know God with far greater understanding of truth that these life-application lessons came to fruition. Through many difficult and challenging trials, God revealed to me just how absorbed I had become with so many musical-, teaching-, and performance-related distractions. God knew what was best in permitting the stripping away of those very things that were so prominently keeping me away from being able to glorify and honor Him acceptably.

Worship of God has been a focal point in my life over the past two decades, which has resulted in my having read numerous books and online publications regarding the culture of worship within the church. I've also engaged in innumerable conversations with people from various denominations within the Christian sphere, from ultraconservative to exceedingly contemporary, and those in between. These combined experiences, along with my personal observations in having visited several evangelical churches over the years, have resulted in many profound eye-opening insights.

I've come to realize that I'm not alone and most certainly not the first person to be convicted of what many believe is becoming a widely unspoken epidemic within a vast number of evangelical churches. Specifically that is to say, in our having turned from biblical worship worthy unto God to having pursued popularity among the masses. Perhaps this is in part because far too many have turned a deaf ear to the specific barriers that significantly hinder their times of worship, obstruct the work of the Holy Spirit, and repress the genuine experience of revival.

The cultural norm of the church has collectively reversed over the years as a significant number of pastors have turned their focus of approval outwardly to that of the congregation, rather than upwardly toward Christ Jesus in the planning of their services. Many leaders within the church body have now shifted toward delivering messages that will appeal to the seeker, rather than teaching and preaching the truth of God's whole Word. Likewise, a significant number of the songs chosen each week for intended worship of God are being selected by means of popularity among the people, rather than those that most glorify, exalt, and magnify God's true righteousness.

The tragic results of these pandemic phenomena are the rapid increase of spiritual apathy and irreverence of many proclaimed believers toward the righteousness and holiness of the deity of almighty God.

During the process of writing this book, I met on several occasions with a guy by the name of Dan Foley. Dan is a most treasured friend of nearly thirty years and is also a wonderful pastor and worship leader. I asked him if he'd be willing to review my drafts as they progressed and provide me with his feedback and insights. Graciously he accepted and I am honored he did! During one of our times in getting together and discussing the development of this book, Dan told me something that pierced into the fabric of my soul. One of the things he said to me was, "We must always treat the church as Christ's bride." His words came at a perfect time and truly were God sent!

As I refer to the church within this book, I do so with no intention of depicting any particular denomination or specific group of believers. All true believers in Christ Jesus collectively make up the church body, Christ's church, which is His bride. With this in mind, I hope you will receive the words on the subsequent pages, from the heart with which they are written. Filled with utmost concern, passion, and an eagerness for revival to break forth among all believers, I fervently trust God to open our eyes and ears to the truth of His Word, and that through such unveiling, we will purpose to seek His manifest glory among us!

Now, before you read any further, I ask that you'd pause a moment and prayerfully seek the Holy Spirit, asking Him to challenge and convict you into all biblical and spiritual truth.

My prayer for us is that collectively we might become a radiant and holy bride, shining the light of Christ Jesus unto a darkened world. That we neither compromise nor cover God's truth in order to be accepted, but rather purpose to be convicted to change for His glory!

Chapter 4

An Awakening to Revival of Holy Worship

Back in 2008, my wife, Monica, and I were about to celebrate our twenty-fifth wedding anniversary. We'd never been to Europe and found an incredible two-week cruise being offered. We also decided to stay a week in Paris, as we had no idea if or when we might return. After our first week on the cruise, we came to Rome, Italy. Having the entire day there, we tried to see as much as possible. During our tour, we had about an hour to walk through St. Peter's Basilica church in Vatican City.

The size of the building was almost beyond comprehension, and I remember being overwhelmed at all of the paintings and statuary. I felt I could spend days inside trying to absorb all there was to see. The length is approximately seven hundred feet, and it is in the shape of a Latin cross. But what stood out to me more than anything at the moment were the ceilings. They were so high; they just seemed so far out of reach. I remember thinking, *How could anyone possibly get up there to paint or do any work at all for that matter?*

Now being transparent with you here, I recall vividly being a little put off by how truly mind-boggling the church was to me. St. Peter's can hold about sixty thousand people for a mass, and it covers an area over 163,000 feet inside. I would be untruthful if I didn't say that at that moment in time, I felt it was a bit pretentious. As Monica and I continued to walk about and I was taking pictures as fast as I could, I felt taken aback by a feeling of there being an ostentatious display of human works. It was just so hard to take it all in—the grandiose trimmings of such piercing colors, and those ceilings ... I mean, they were just so stupid high to me. Trying to look up gave me a headache, and I was thinking to myself, *Why did they have to make the ceilings so ridiculously high?*

Within moments of those feelings and internal questions, I would discover the answers; why so many of the churches that we were about to visit throughout Europe were built in such a similar fashion. Now, I don't recall if this information came to me via the tour guide or by written material, but what I learned was so impacting to me that I could hardly seek forgiveness from God fast enough.

The relevance in the purposeful design of St. Peter's and other such magnificent cathedrals (as I'd soon discover), like St. Mark's Basilica in Venice, Italy, and Notre Dame in Paris, was to establish the greatness of God within the physical structure. Upon walking in through the doorways, one is to look upward as to heaven, to gaze in awe, wonder, and reverence.

The towering height is purposeful to remind each person who entered into God's house of His majesty and splendor, of how significant God is and just how little we are compared to His immensity. They're designed to take our breath away, not as a result of the adorned human works, achievements, or for their accolades, but rather, because of our absolute astonishment of God's perfect holiness, character, and attributes!

Those churches provide a radiant reminder for all who enter, a prompting and call for authentic humility in the presence of the Holy Trinity of God—one that we should possess at all times.

That's a lesson right there, friend, and let me tell you, it's one I hope to never forget. Regardless of any building I enter for the purpose of assembly with other believers to glorify God, any time I pray or offer praise unto Him, I seek to always have that same feeling of utter awe, humility, and reverence toward God.

A person would be hard-pressed to find a more profound exclamation of reverence toward God then that of the words of St. Augustine. I hope you'll read the following text slowly, deliberately, and with great reflection:

> What art Thou then, my God? What, but the Lord God? For who is Lord but the Lord? Or who is God save our God? Most highest, most good, most potent, most omnipotent; most merciful, yet most just; most hidden, yet most present; most beautiful, yet most strong, stable, yet incomprehensible; unchangeable, yet all-changing; never new, never old; all-renewing, and bringing age upon the proud, and they know it not; ever working, ever at rest; still gathering, yet nothing lacking; supporting, filling, and overspreading; creating, nourishing, and maturing; seeking, yet having all things. Thou lovest, without passion; art jealous, without anxiety; repentest, yet grievest not; art angry,

yet serene; changest Thy works, Thy purpose unchanged; receivest again what Thou findest, yet didst never lose; never in need, yet rejoicing in gains; never covetous, yet exacting usury. Thou receivest over and above, that Thou mayest owe; and who hath aught that is not Thine? Thou payest debts, owing nothing; remittest debts, losing nothing. And what had I now said, my God, my life, my holy joy? or what saith any man when he speaks of Thee? Yet woe to him that speaketh not, since mute are even the most eloquent.[2]

A Definition of Biblical Holy Worship:

We should acknowledge God's worthiness of all honor, praise, and glory. As we mature in our faith, our response will be to live continually in humility, obedience, devotion, and adoration of God the Father, Christ Jesus the Son, and the Holy Spirit, the triunity of God Almighty!

> Saints are described as fearing the name of God; they are reverent worshippers; they stand in awe of the Lord's authority; they are afraid of offending Him; they feel their own nothingness in the sight of the Infinite One.[3]

---

2 Saint Augustine (354–430), *The Confessions of St. Augustine*, book I, chapter IV.
3 Charles Haddon Spurgeon, *The Treasury of David*, Psalm 61:5.

Section 2

The Prominent Barriers Obstructing Holy Worship

Chapter 5

The Barrier of Unholy Irreverence

Within these next few pages, I hope to engage your thoughts to reflect upon the ensuing questions. They're specifically intended for you to truthfully ponder their relevance to your personal experiences and observations. I submit the following with no intention of being hypercritical. Rather, I intend to encourage your most deliberate, truthful contemplation.

When was the last time you attended a church service and were so deeply moved by the workings of the Holy Spirit that you didn't want to leave when the service was finished?

When was the last time you personally experienced the manifold presence of God during a Christian gathering, where lives were being shook, transformed, and restored? Where the congregation lingered long after the gathering had concluded?

When was the last time you recall showing up for church ten to fifteen minutes early and praying for God to "show up" and reveal Himself to you personally and to others within the congregation?

Now, I ask you to consider the following for a moment:

How often do the very people who call themselves Christians, those who profess to be committed followers of Christ, show up significantly early in order to "tailgate" at football games and other major sporting events? They commit to such plans several days and even weeks prior to get there early for a good parking spot to celebrate with friends long before the actual event ever begins.

How frequently do those same people arrive twenty to thirty minutes early to the movies and with their drinks, popcorn, and candies in hand sit through several minutes of advertisements and previews, long before the featured film begins? And upon the conclusion, they leave while the credits for the film roll by on the screen. I suspect many of these same people are the ones who leave a service as the last song is being offered up to God, treating the ending moments of a worship service similar to that of a movie's ending acknowledgments: "Let's leave and beat the crowd out the door."

Then there are the concertgoers, the fans of the bands who with tremendous anticipation count down the days until they are in the presence of their favorite performers. Often, those same people who attend these performances will stand for hours on end, actively participating in loud singing, dancing, and thunderous applause in utter idolization.

I ask you to consider your punctuality at the place where you're employed. How about your consideration for others when meeting for coffee, lunches, or joining them for dinner?

Now, stop and think about how many people arrive to the house of the Lord God late.

Imagine if you will: the service has begun, the worship team is long into perhaps several songs, and people are still straggling into the service. Those who arrived early, now have to move about to accommodate the seating of those who are tardy. Their personal communion with God having been disrupted, it can sometimes take an entire song or more before they're settled back into the place of meditating upon the glories of God.

How has this happened? How have we become so lethargic in our arriving to the house of the Lord? Why have we lost so much of the spiritual fervency and excitement that once was held so dear, by so many?

Congregations most often will follow their pastors, with a tendency to emulate the spiritual authorities who lead them in all areas of ministry. If the pastoral team fails to preach God's Word in its entirety, you can be assured the congregation will possess a diminished perspective of biblical truth. Spiritual capacity can only be filled by spiritual competency.

With eyes wide open with intent to observe, it's glaringly apparent we've become a nation of tolerance and acceptance. And it's with many of those same accommodating mind-sets that we've embraced an "it's all good" attitude that now permeates so many of our worship places. Far from the norm are the evangelical churches, which hold firmly to sound biblical doctrine of the Christian faith. Far too few in leadership promote and biblically instruct their congregations about godly reverence and holy acceptable worship offered to God.

Can we really have become so callused of heart that we could possibly believe that anything we offer up to God is "all good"?

Have we been so inundated with new teachings and ideologies that under God's grace, we feel we can arrive to the Lord's house whenever and however we want to and the Almighty will be thrilled that we bothered to show up at all?

Here are a couple of biblical examples for us to consider:

Perhaps we've forgotten that Cain, the first son of Adam and Eve, was guilty of offering such unacceptable sacrifices and God was not pleased. Cain thought less of God's attributes and failed to look at God in His true character and holiness. Cain thought he could approach God on his own merit and terms and needed no intermediary. Further, he failed to view sin in the same way God looks at sin. He truly believed his actions weren't a big deal and he could do whatever he wanted.

Yet, if we looked within this same story found in Genesis chapter 4, we discover Cain's brother Abel. He knew just what God desired as a sacrifice. Abel was all about offering up to God that which God would find pleasing, holy, and acceptable. And God found regard for Abel's actions, his offering and worship ... but not so with Cain.

> Now Adam knew Eve his wife, and she conceived and bore Cain, and said, "I have acquired a man from the Lord." Then she bore again, this time his brother Abel. Now Abel was a keeper of sheep, but Cain was a tiller of the ground. And in the process of time it came to pass that Cain brought an offering of the fruit of the ground to the Lord. Abel also brought of the firstborn of his flock and of their fat. And the Lord respected Abel and his offering, but He did not respect Cain and his offering.
>
> (Genesis 4:1–5 NKJV)

> By faith Abel offered to God a more excellent sacrifice than Cain.
>
> (Hebrews 11:4 NKJV)

David is another tremendous example! His life's testimony throughout the Old Testament books is filled with the lessons he learned regarding rightful worship due unto the Lord God Almighty. Over the course of his life, he wrote much about his experiences throughout the Psalms. One of my favorites comes from Psalm 51:10-12, 15-17. I can't begin to express how paramount these verses are toward the development of a true worshipper of God. When we approach the throne of God with all humility, a truly broken spirit, and with a heart of contrition in those areas of our lives that are unpleasing before God, then He is able to do His work in us and through us.

> Create in me a clean heart O God, and renew a steadfast spirit within me. Do not cast me away from Your presence, and do not take Your Holy Spirit from me. Restore to me the joy of Your salvation, and uphold me by Your generous Spirit ... O Lord, open my lips, and my mouth shall show forth Your praise. For you do not desire sacrifice, or else I would give it; You do not delight in burnt offering. The sacrifices of God are a broken spirit, a broken and contrite heart—these O God, you will not despise.
>
> (Psalm 51:10-12, 15-17 NKJV)

In our recognizing that Abel's sacrifice was better than his brother's and knowing God is immutable (Malachi 3:6; Hebrews 13:8), shouldn't this inspire our hearts to seek forgiveness, repenting of our lackadaisical approach and thereby beseech God to restore our times of praise to be a sweet aroma of adoration unto Him?

The Construction of the Barrier of Irreverence

This barrier of irreverence and disrespectfulness has been a long work in progress over the decades and even centuries within the church, one that has been built up brick by brick as a result of what I believe are two primary causes. The first cause is *spiritual ignorance*. Most people just don't know any better and most of them were never taught how to truly worship God correctly. The second cause stems from being *spiritually arrogant*. Much like Cain, a significant number of people look at God's grace as a license to approach His holy presence any way they choose, offering whatever they feel like.

Before one can begin to worship God with humbleness and holiness of heart, a proper relational understanding toward God is of absolute necessity. Allow yourself to examine with purposeful reflection the truth to be discovered within the following text from A. W. Tozer's *The Pursuit of God*.

> Every soul belongs to God and exists by His pleasure. God being Who and What He is, and we being who and what we are, the only thinkable relation between us is one of full lordship on His part and complete submission on ours. We owe Him every honor that it is in our power to give Him. Our everlasting grief lies in giving Him anything less.[4]

Taking Responsibility for Our Actions

One of my favorite passages in the Bible comes from the book of Nehemiah. In the first chapter, we discover the walls of the city of Jerusalem had been broken down and the gates were destroyed

---

[4] A. W. Tozer, *The Pursuit of God* (public domain, 1948).

by fire. Nehemiah wept and was in mourning for many days when the news was told to him regarding the condition of Jerusalem.

Yet, look at how he responded. The first thing he did was pray to God. He poured out his heart in confession and repentance and pleaded for God to allow him to rebuild the wall and gates of the city. In the second chapter, we find him going out at nighttime to survey all of the damage in order to fully understand the magnitude of what needed to be restored.

In contrast to the burden and challenges Nehemiah faced in rebuilding the walls and gates of Jerusalem, we need to have the very barriers we've built up, torn down. As our first priority in seeking to have those obstacles removed, we should deliberately follow his example. And that, my friend, is through prayer!

We can learn a great deal from the testimony of this man's life. We, too, should cry out to God, confessing our sins in having forsaken His Word and instructions for the rightful worship He is due, and so worthy thereof. We should repent of having allowed an all-too-familiar demeanor of irreverence and casualness to preside over our having humility, reverence, and fearful awe of the Lord our God.

In such times of our communion with God, we can take great confidence that the prayer offered in faith and truth will be heard. For He remains faithful even when we are not! We can rest assured that we will be shown the barriers around us, those obstacles that have become hindrances to our times of worship. God will reveal through His Holy Spirit that which needs to be leveled and the debris needing to be removed.

Chapter 6

THE ENTRAPMENT OF ENTERTAINMENT

> But the hour is coming, and now is, when the true worshipers will worship the Father in spirit and truth; for the Father is seeking such to worship Him.
>
> (John 4:23 NKJV)

In our current culture, we've become overtly focused upon being entertained with lighting effects, visually stimulating backdrops, not to mention theatrics of all sorts. And we view mega-screens that ten years ago didn't exist even in major sporting venues. We've brought the worldly effects into the church to stimulate our senses, and in the process we've driven out the working of the Holy Spirit through our own self-sufficient euphoric engineered experiences.

Before I became deaf, I remember people expressing concerns of their various experiences regarding times of worship. Often referring to the production aspects of the program being viewed as nothing more than "emotional manipulation." Let's face the fact, that we've become experts at the production of worship, the engineering and manufacturing of stimulating the senses. We've brought the worldly "tricks of the trade" into forming programs resulting in appeal to a secular-induced euphoria. These are based upon the strategic stimulation of both visual and hearing senses, which is nothing more than cheap entertainment.

The temptation to tickle the ears and entertain the eyes with muses that appease the masses is nothing new. Yet, most tragically, it's become significantly more abrasive with a blurring of the truth in both doctrine and biblical worship. I urge you to consider the following prophetic insights from two tremendous preachers of God's Word:

> A time will come when instead of shepherds feeding the sheep, the church will have clowns entertaining the goats.
>
> —C. H. Spurgeon
>
> Religion today is not transforming the people—it is being transformed by the people. It is not raising the moral level of society—it is descending to society's own level and congratulating itself that it has scored a victory because society is smiling accepting its surrender.
>
> —A. W. Tozer

At the risk of being redundant here, let me state it again. Like Nehemiah, we would do well to assess all the areas that lie in ruins, plan to sift through the rubble, and then be about our Lord's business in pursuing the restoration of righteous standing, the worth of our adoration and praise due unto God Almighty!

Evangelical churches, which strive to be socially acceptable to the masses, cannot be theologically correct in worship. Those who cannot worship in spirit and truth will look to be entertained by various offered amusements and numerous activities. They will seek theatrics and secularities to appease the void of an authentic worship experience, whereby God inhabits the praises of His people. The absence of the Holy Spirit at work within a local body of believers will never be replaced by even the most elaborate endeavors of man. There is no appeasement apart from the holy presence of God. Let's own up to the truth: worldly entertainment with all its socially acceptable moral decay has absolutely no place in the house of almighty God!

I believe that the basis of authentic worship can best be described as an acknowledgment of belonging to God; recognizing His perfect and holy attributes, which ascribes to the worthiness, honor, thanksgiving, and praises due unto Him. In our personal relationship with God through the indwelling of the Holy Spirit, genuine true worship comes forth from our hearts, minds, and souls filled with humility, obedience, and adoration to God the Father, Christ Jesus the Son, and the Holy Spirit.

However, this is often not the case during many of the modern-day Christian worship services occurring across our nation. Think of how often you've heard people complain about the choice of songs or the person who sang the song or the clothes they were wearing; whether a person was wearing too much makeup or not enough; that the music was too loud or not loud enough; that the church was too conservative or not contemporary enough; that the service was too boring or overboard on stimulation... and the list goes on. In all candidness, I've been guilty at times of such sentiments and complaints as well. It is high time we recognize, that such attitudes of the heart are far from worshipping in spirit and in truth!

I came across the following sermon excerpt of Charles Spurgeon, which he preached in 1892. His words should compel us to utmost consideration and inspire us into appropriate actions:

> If we add to our churches by becoming worldly, by taking in persons who have never been born again; if we add to our churches by accommodating the life of the Christian to the life of the worldling, our increase is worth nothing at all; it is a loss rather than a gain! If we add to our churches by excitement, by making appeals to the passions rather than by explaining the truth of God to the understanding; if we add to our churches otherwise than by the power of the Spirit of God making men new creatures in Christ Jesus, the increase is of no worth whatever![5]

We are at a time within the church where we desperately need to return to the true heart of worship! As a body of believers, we must purposefully forgo the ideologies of entertainment being the method of creating excitement toward God. It's imperative for our Christian leaders to turn away from that of seeking congregational appeasement and lead us back into following Christ's command, to "worship in spirit and in truth"!

---

5   C. H. Spurgeon, Metropolitan Tabernacle Pulpit, Sermon 2265 (1892).

Chapter 7

The Obstruction of Production

One of the more powerful and painful lessons that God revealed to me during my season as a worship leader was the fact that I spent significantly more time being focused on the *production of worship*, than I did on the *person of worship*. Plain and simple, I was much more concerned about the musical greatness and esoteric effects in trying to manipulate a spiritual experience than I was about simplifying the music and allowing God to be adored through personal authenticity.

In my serving within various ministries over the past three decades, I've observed a troubling number of churches that have become promoters of popular programs and people rather than prophets of God's Word, houses of prayer, or places of authentic biblical worship. We need to acknowledge that God needs neither endorsements of celebrities or human agents of approval.

God is God, the great I AM. He is self-existing, all-powerful, and without beginning or end. We need not bother looking out for approval from others. We need only to look up to God and seek His presence in holy reverence for Him to manifest Himself to us. God is omniscient and there is no place He is not. However, His manifest presence happens when we sense His presence and see the Holy Spirit at work in the lives of believers. That is the defining difference and it can't be manipulated, manufactured, or engineered!

> I wonder if there was ever a time when true spiritual worship was at a lower ebb. To great sections of the church, the art of worship has been lost entirely, and in its place has come that strange and foreign thing called the "program." This word has been borrowed from the stage and applied with sad wisdom to the public service which now passes for worship among us.[6]

Neither timidity nor tolerance will suffice as the necessary tools needed for removing this most dangerous barrier within the church. We need to ask God for a spiritual sledgehammer and the strength to begin to swing away.

> Do not love the world or the things in the world. If anyone loves the world, the love of the Father is not in him. For all that is in the world—the lust of the flesh, the lust of the eyes, and the pride of life—is not of the Father but is of the world.
>
> (1 John 2:15–16 NKJV)

---

6   A.W. Tozer

Chapter 8

THE IMPEDIMENT OF ME

Another tender lesson of truth God revealed to me was that of the "self" or "I" barriers: the massive obstructions of me, myself, and I. That triple threat was obstructing the very worship in which I was participating and expectantly hopeful to receive a blessed experience. You see, over the years, I had built up several self-expectations of what I thought needed to happen within a worship setting. Further, there was my ideology of self-engagement. In other words, having this predisposition of, "What's going to keep me effectively engaged?" "What gets me going, fired-up, motivated, and enthusiastic … and are those who are leading going to make it happen?"

It's like I was heading into God's house with an attitude of, "I sure hope the service is going to be good and I get something out of it." I had no focus upon making it a priority of worshipping God rightfully on many of those Sundays, and through God unveiling my self-indulgent thinking I realized that I was merely seeking to be entertained, one way or another, be it via the preaching, or the overall program.

This was specifically true in the area of musical worship. The vast majority of my thoughts were focused upon the songs I liked, the people whose voices I wanted to hear singing, the right mix of the sound I thought was acceptable ... not too loud for vocals, more drums, more guitar, less keyboards, more bass ... what I thought was best for God to hear for His glorification. Can you imagine the audacity of me? Now, I'm not saying here that a good musical mix isn't important, because the reality is, an uneducated soundperson can ruin the musical/vocal performances if they don't know what they're doing, and it can truly dampen the entire experience of musical worship.

In all of this, there was a critical message for me to understand: worship isn't about me, myself, or I. It has nothing to do with what I prefer or desire! The songs being offered aren't about me whatsoever. They're intended for God and His glory alone! And let me say something else here, to which my eyes were opened up to see. That genuine holy, pleasing, and acceptable worship to God is not about if I'm in the mood or feeling the right emotions for my enjoyment. I can recall, it was as though God was saying, "Those songs aren't for your pleasure, Tim, they're for My praise!" Ouch! That was a huge lesson for me to learn! I really like the way Dan wrote it out on a notepad and passed it to me one day at lunch, while talking about this chapter: "It's not about me, it's about He." I can't honestly begin to image how often I used to crash into the obstacle of "me" when it came to the worship of "He." Let me ask you something: Are you perhaps feeling a bit of a tug of truth here? Just checking.

> Whenever the living creatures give glory and honor and thanks to Him who sits on the throne,

who lives forever and ever, the twenty-four elders fall down before Him who sits on the throne and worship Him who lives forever and ever, and cast their crowns before the throne, saying: "You are worthy, O Lord, To receive glory and honor and power; For You created all things, And by Your will they exist and were created.

(Revelation 4:9–11 NKJV)

Chapter 9

The By-Product Protrusion

Let me present two facts for your consideration.

1. A church of Christ can have biblically sound doctrine in its teaching and yet hold an incorrect methodology in its practices of worshipping God.

2. We can tell a great deal about what a church believes from the songs they sing.

A church with a holy reverence toward God and His true character will be reflected in their time of worship. We must take to heart that God's Word is to be presented in its entire truth in order to make us better worshippers. We've gotten the whole thing wrong for the most part! Most people believe they worship through the singing of songs in church in order to quiet their spirit, as a means to prepare them to receive the Word of God. That's often a by-product of worship, but not the purpose. When it comes to the prioritization of *what before why*, we must take hold of the following biblical truth: *we study the Word of God in order to become better worshippers of God!*

As we purpose to study the whole Word of God, we will continually discover greater depths of truth. In doing so, we will mature in our faith, the Holy Spirit creating within us the desire to live a worshipful, God-honoring life. From apprehending truth-filled knowledge, we progress toward application—wisdom in action, resulting in continual praise, prayer, and submission to God's leading throughout our daily affairs. The Word of God is totally sufficient for all of Christian living! There is no guesswork to be considered when contemplating how we are to become better worshippers. God's Word is clear for those whose true intent is to live for Him, His glory and exaltation.

The Reverend Assembly of Divines at Westminster came to agree that "man's chief end is to glorify God and enjoy Him forever." That is our ultimate destiny in our relationship with God: to glorify, worship, and enjoy being in the presence of God for all eternity. This is supported by the revelation given to John while exiled on Patmos. The angels worship God continually, without end. Notice, there is no message or vision of our having to continually study God's Word or participate in any form of continued academic studies occurring in heaven. God will fully reveal all truth to us when we are with Him. His Word will be implanted into all our being and from this, we will unceasingly worship Him in all spirit and truth.

Now, I want to challenge us as a community of believers to examine why so many of us are caught in a rut ... a perpetual programming of our worship services. In my forty plus years of attending various evangelical worship services, from Nazarene, Methodist, Wesleyan, Baptist, and several nondenominational churches, I can tell you unequivocally that they all (without exception) followed a repetitive pattern for conducting a worship service: welcome, worship songs, announcements, offering, message, last song, service concludes. Okay, so stop here and check me on this to see if this is what is going on in your church service experiences as well.

Don't misunderstand me on this matter as I'm not saying this is wrong, but I will go out on a limb here and state that this pattern works well for the latecomers to show up and not disrupt the preacher's message. However, this repetitive pattern puts us more in a spiritual rut than a spiritual revival.

In the New Testament, I discovered a fascinating scriptural approach to apply to our times of worship. Some people will claim there is very little written within the New Testament as to the order of how we're to conduct our worship services. Paul wrote about our times of gathering being orderly and without confusion or disruptive outbursts. Yet, I want to take us to a book in the Bible that I believe could serve us well as a newfound template toward promoting revival. I'm not suggesting we do away with the forgoing format we all are so accustomed to, but I am strongly encouraging those who plan out the worship service to shake things up a bit and not allow a programmed stagnation to rule our times of assembly to worship God.

With that I take us to the last book of the Bible, Revelation, which contains the last messages and prophecies from Christ Jesus revealed to John. While deep in the study of end-times prophecies and current worldly events, my attention was drawn to a most fascinating revelation (no pun intended)!

In reading through chapters 1 through 3, you'll find that Christ gave His message of warning to the seven churches of Asia Minor. In chapter 4 verses 8 through 11 and chapter 5, we are drawn to John's witness of worship in heaven. Then we come to chapter 6, another vision and message to be recorded, followed by worship in chapter 7. Chapters 8 through 10 contain more visions and messages, and then John's testimony of witnessing more heavenly worship is in chapter 11. This pattern follows all the way through the book of Revelation: a message accompanied with a vision and then worship. In Revelation 22:8–9, the last chapter in the last book of the Bible, we're told to "keep the words of this book. Worship God."

Let me direct us to the writing of J. Vernon McGee on this passage:

> John was so impressed that his natural reaction was to fall down and worship the angel. The simplicity and meekness of the angel are impressive. Though the angels were created above man, this angel identifies himself as a fellow servant with John and the other prophets. He was merely a messenger to communicate God's Word to man, and he directs all worship to God. Christ is the centerpiece of the Book of Revelation—don't lose sight of Him.

The Word, the message, the revelation of God, should lead us to the worship of God. It is the Word of God that brings us to the holy worship of God!

Chapter 10

THE CHECKPOINT OF CONSUMERISM

If we truly desire to experience the manifest presence of God in our times of gathering, then we must recognize the specific barriers within our churches. Worshipping in truth demands for us to look how besieged so many of our churches have become with a consumerism approach toward drawing people to the house of God. In other words, "give the people what they what, not what they need." Unlike the character of James Bond in the movies when ordering his favorite drink, we should seek to be both *shaken* and *stirred* by the Word and presence of God and the convicting power of the Holy Spirit.

Consumerism in the church demands meeting the needs of the people rather than the requirements of God. It forces a mind-set of offering church in a "best deal" ideology, providing those who attend "church in a box" with expediency and minimal effort. It's all good, quick, easy, and painless. Let's not fool ourselves! God-honoring glorification can never be received by such means!

From the *entrapments of entertainment* to the light-hearted messages being preached from the pulpit, people have grown accustomed to being comforted above being convicted. People for the most part don't want to leave church having been stirred up in their souls, realizing a need to repent of certain sins and confess that which grieves the Holy Spirit and suppresses God's work. Many a believer today wants the celebratory songs with rhythm, hand clapping, and foot stomping over those songs that would drive us to our knees before the almighty God.

There are a vast number of pastors who week in and week out are boxed into a corner, facing the demands of a threatening voting board or congregation that dictates the church's culture with a consumerism feel-good approach. Rather than being focused on a worship service by teaching the Word of God in its entirety and to worship God in a most holy and pleasing manner unto Him, these ministers are burdened with thoughts of, "What will my board or members think?"

I'm talking about those passages of God's Word that point directly to the heart of our sins and demand our utmost attention … the sins of immoral sexuality, coveting, comparison, idolatry, vanity, gluttony, and those of self-sins. How utterly heart wrenching this must be for the man of God who once was so passionately devoted to shepherd the flock but now finds himself forced to produce a program, fashionable with the people.

Consumerism in the church is most evidenced when the church promotes all the programs they offer to attract people, as opposed to the Word of God being taught with authenticity and in whole. Such gatherings of believers solely look to their activities to draw people, rather than the power of God drawing those to His place of worship. The ever-frequent dialogue is geared toward amusing programs and connecting-point activities instead of the Word being taught and the testimony of conversions and disciples being made all to God's glory and workings within the church.

> But my people have forgotten me; they make offerings to false gods; they make them stumble in their ways.
>
> (Jeremiah 18:15 ESV)
>
> Do not be conformed to this world, but be transformed by the renewal of your mind, that by testing you may discern what is the will of God, what is good and acceptable and perfect.
>
> (Romans 12:2 ESV)

Chapter 11

The Cost Deterrent of Worship

Genuine worship requires both effort and discipline of heart, mind, and soul. With significant forethought, we must endeavor to block out the distractions of life, which often creep into our times of glorifying God. We must realize true worship happens not one day a week, but rather seven days per week. How we praise God on Monday counts the same as what we did on Sunday. There are persons equipped with a plethora of excuses to stay bedside on Sunday, that they'd never dream of using as such reasoning for not showing up to work on Monday.

We should strive to be living worshipful lives in joyful praise, thanksgiving, and adoration at all times—not just a few hours per week. God is looking at the quality of the hearts within the church, not the quantity of the congregation in the seats or pews.

Worship that exalts and blesses God can never come by means of ritual, repetition, or through being reluctant. That was the problem of the Old Testament church. Matthew Henry referred to those who worshipped by such means as being both "clouded and clogged." He also encouraged us that we, "must worship Him with fixedness of thought and a flame of affection, with all that is within us."[7]

I believe there is a prominent difference between those who approach worship with typical tendencies and those with a transparent heart. For when the heart, mind, and soul are retrospective, repentant, and reverent, it is there that we meet with God in authenticity and will begin to experience revival and restoration of true fellowship. When we come to the end of ourselves, where we fall on our knees before God, it's there at that point in time and in the reverent posture of heart where genuine adoration and truthful worship begins.

> Therefore, having these promises, beloved, let us cleanse ourselves from all filthiness of the flesh and spirit, perfecting holiness in the fear of God.
>
> (2 Corinthians 7:1 NKJV)

It's high time for us to recognize our casual mind-sets and allow this paramount truth to sink in deep: *worshipping God in spirit and truth will cost us much!* Giving to God out of our convenience of time—that which is left over—is unworthy to offer. We must be willing to sacrifice and give up the pride of our heart, the lust of the eyes and flesh that attempts to draw us away from seeking God's presence. We must yield ourselves to the Spirit and forgo the secular pressures in desiring to be entertained. Yet, no matter how much we sacrifice unto God, the cost will never be more than

---

[7] Matthew Henry, *Matthew Henry's Commentary on the Whole Bible* (public domain).

we can afford to give, when given with humility of heart, mind, and soul.

> For godly sorrow produces repentance leading to salvation, not to be regretted; but the sorrow of the world produces death.
>
> (2 Corinthians 7:10 NKJV)
>
> And whatever you do, do it heartily, as to the Lord and not to men, knowing that from the Lord you will receive the reward of the inheritance; for you serve the Lord Christ.
>
> (Colossians 3:23–24 NKJV)

When I consider the vast multitudes, the thousands upon thousands of people walking through the freezing temperatures in England to hear a message from Charles Spurgeon or through bitter-cold winds of winter in Chicago to listen to a sermon from D. L. Moody, I'm left with the deep sadness that we have lost much of our spiritual fervency and eager expectancy. It appears that the majority of people are no longer willing to endure any personal hardships or inconvenience in hopes of meeting with the Lord God and to experience the transcending power of the Holy Spirit.

Chapter 12

The Musical Mandate Roadblock

I want to introduce you to a term I've adopted to help describe one of the barriers that so greatly hinders the vast majority of people as it relates to worshipping God, and that is *secondhand worship*.

No doubt that phrase might be a bit perplexing and to some, perhaps even somewhat disturbing. However, this was yet another eye-opener (or might I suggest, an *ear-opener*), that God brought to my attention after my inability to hear music, voices, or to compose songs to magnify His name.

Now, let me set the record straight as a precursor to this entire chapter. The concept of secondhand worship is in no way intended to be demeaning or condescending within any intended delineation. Rather, I submit this as a truth we must all recognize!

How this was revealed to me came about through my having written and produced Christian music for many years, including contemporary Christian pop and praise-and-worship songs. Frequently during the rehearsals prior to performing or recording the music, I'd find myself having to explain the lyrics and background of the song. It was important for me to communicate to the musicians and vocalists the story behind the lyrics and to give my personal insights in order to help them greater understand the message and emotion I desired to be conveyed. And the reason for all this was simple! They hadn't written the lyrics or the music. It was my song, my words, from my heart to God. And that's exactly how it is for the vast majority of people every single week during any given worship service. Unless they wrote the lyrics and music, they're singing the words and melody of someone else's created work.

Let me clarify something at this point. This concept is not a negative aspect of worship whatsoever! But it is a truth we all must understand and would do well to embrace. When we sing a melody and lyrics from that which someone else wrote, it's being handed down to us, passed along. We can't argue the fact that the words have been provided to us by someone else; we receive it secondhand.

Let's look at it from another point of view by means of similar comparison.

We might come into possession of a collection of beautifully written, heartfelt love letters from an author to his parents, spouse, children, and most cherished friends. We could copy them, sign our name at the bottom, and pass them along accordingly, but they would always be the words of the originating author and not our own.

Though they may well indeed express our very sentiments of love and perhaps our deepest feelings we desire to communicate, we would have to agree they, in fact, were written by someone else. Tens of millions of greeting cards are sold each year under this same principle. Millions of people are merely giving written expression to the ones they hold dear, the words originally written by another's hand.

Does this mean that if you can't write music or lyrics, you're unfit to worship God? Of course not! Am I trying to insinuate that when we gather together as a body of believers and sing songs of praise unto God, just because someone else wrote the music and lyrics, that it makes us unable worship God effectively? Absolutely not!

So then, how does this apply to our individual and corporate times of worship? Watch this now and take time to really understand where I'm heading!

There is a very simple biblical truth for each of us to comprehend and contend with as part of our daily lives and I'm going to state it here and then present the validity of this truth as found in God's Word. I ask you to read the following slowly and a few times through ... let it really sink in deep: *Worshipping God is not a musical mandate!*

> He may worship God who shouts until the earth rings, and God may accept him. But he may worship God as truly who sits in silence before the Most High and says not even a word. It is the spiritual worship, which is most acceptable to God, not the external in any shape or form. It is the heart that has fellowship with the Lord, and it needs little in the way of expressing itself—neither has God tied it down to this way or that. It may find its own methods of utterance so long as it is truly "moved by the Holy Spirit."[8]

---

8   Charles Haddon Spurgeon, Sermon 2239 (1892).

If you stop and ask someone to define what it means to outwardly worship God, their answer most commonly will detail worship being equated with music and singing. In our culture today, among the many denominations in the United States, worship and music can hardly be differentiated. Even among those who have studied God's Word in depth over the years, they naturally seem to gravitate to the specific text that identifies worship and singing, and praises being sung to God, going hand in hand. This is true with many of the Psalms, as we find within the headings of many modern translations the original direction calling for musical accompaniment.

If we take the above into consideration, coupled with the current limited teachings relating to biblical worship coming from the pulpit, we find ourselves stuck in the middle of synonymously equating worship with music. The truth is that in our current contemporary service formats, they're virtually inseparable.

This however is a false assumption, and the misconception has resulted in a vast number of congregations suffering from an incorrect theological application. It's imperative for us to learn that there are significant numbers of Scripture that provide great details of the worship of God without music ever having been a part.

Many of the Psalms that were written giving praise, glory, and thanksgiving to God were words from the heart of the author with no musical accompaniment intended. We can also look to Christ's revelation to John. Consider just the following two passages, which provide evidence of the fact of this biblical truth:

> The four living creatures, each having six wings, were full of eyes around and within. And they do not rest day or night, saying: "Holy, holy, holy, Lord God Almighty, Who was and is and is to come!" Whenever the living creatures give glory and

honor and thanks to Him who sits on the throne, who lives forever and ever, the twenty-four elders fall down before Him who sits on the throne and worship Him who lives forever and ever, and cast their crowns before the throne, saying: "You are worthy, O Lord, To receive glory, honor and power; For You created all things, And by Your will they exist and were created."

(Revelation 4:8–11 NKJV)

Then I looked, and I heard the voice of many angels around the throne, the living creatures, and the elders; and the number of them was ten thousand times then thousand, and thousands of thousands, saying with a loud voice: "worthy is the Lamb who was slain to receive power and riches and wisdom, And strength and honor and glory and blessing!"

(Revelation 5:11–14 NKJV)

Did you happen to notice within these verses how the glorification and exaltation of God was transpiring? Look closely and you'll discover that John details exactly what was happening ... the six-winged creatures and the twenty-four elders, along with the heavenly host of multitudes were "saying" the words in their praises, not singing the words. This is so critically important for us to comprehend! Because when we get our heads around this truth, we'll understand that we can join in with the thousands times ten thousands voices of heaven, anytime, anyplace, and just proclaim the heavenly praises echoing among the angelic host, and participate in giving glory to God.

I really hope you'll grab hold of this truth: We don't need music! We don't need to know how to play an instrument! We're not required to have a certain level of vocal capability for singing—

or to have any other skills for that matter! Just the words pouring forth from our hearts before the Father, in spirit and truth ... that's worship!

Let me remind you that the Bible is filled with evidence of the heavenly hosts and their proclamations of their praises unto God, in *saying* the words not *singing* them. I believe part of the problem for us today stems from our having literally thousands of songs produced where the lyrics we sing have come directly from biblical passages. This leaves most people to assume it was intended as a song, a lyric to be sung, rather than simply text to be studied.

We desperately need to get away from the correlation of worship always being musical in nature. Why is this so important? Because what I've learned and am passionately committed to teaching and encouraging others to realize is that within each of us there's a God-given ability to create personal worship unto Him. Each person can write or speak forth from his or her heart the words he or she desires to express to God—words of praise, heartfelt devotion, thanksgiving, repentance, joy—and fill pages upon pages of sweet adoration unto God. These are the words we can express from our souls that no other being here on earth may ever hear, sing, or proclaim, yet which the multitudes of heavenly hosts will echo throughout eternity.

Now, think about that for a moment and let that just simmer awhile.

Ten Thousand Times Ten Thousand

Ten thousand times ten thousand in sparking raiment bright
The armies of the ransomed saints throng up the steeps of light;
  'Tis finished, all is finished, their fight with death and sin;
  Fling open wide the golden gates, and let the victors in.

  What rush of alleluias fills all the earth and sky!
What ringing of a thousand harps bespeaks the triumph nigh!
  O day, for which creation and all its tribes were made;
  O joy, for all its former woes a thousand-fold repaid!

  O then what raptured greetings on Canaan's happy shore;
What meeting there of parted friends where partings are no more!
Then eyes with joy shall sparkle, that brimmed with tears of late;
  Orphans no longer fatherless, nor widows desolate.[9]

---

9 "Ten Thousand Times Ten Thousand," lyrics by Henry Alford (1867).

Chapter 13

THE BARRICADE OF COMPARISON

As mentioned previously, I'm still on this journey, not even close to having arrived, and I won't until I'm with Christ. Yet, meanwhile I find myself learning, growing, and being challenged and inspired to convey to those around me the truths that God is teaching me along the way. In all candor and vulnerability here, the barrier of comparison has personally been a huge obstacle for me over the years, and not just when it comes to my glorifying God. The truth be told, *comparison* has been something I've had to contend with for the greater part of my life.

Throughout my musical endeavors, nearly three decades consisted of being a professional musician. During that time, I saw "comparison" as a most valuable tool for studying music. It became engrained into my core being for my style of studying, by comparing myself to see if what I was playing was the same as what was to be learned. Then it progressed into a comparison against other drummers, as this was my main performing instrument. Am I a better drummer than that guy? Do I have a better drum solo than that drummer? Do I have more flash and stage presence? One comparison after another, they mounted up into what eventually became for me a quite formable list.

I was only fourteen years of age when I began playing professionally, and so, that type of mentality in using comparison for study sure seemed innocent enough. And for the most part, it was and it served me very well! However, I had no one holding me accountable, and as I grew older, unfortunately that ideology and worldly philosophy took over and became an internal measuring instrument. In time, I would learn the painful truth that I had become obsessed with self-comparison in most every area of my life.

In my experiences with most people who are openly honest, they too often admit their own struggle with the barrier of comparison to one degree or another. For those folks who might not admit it openly, their comparison thinking is often easily identifiable from their conversations involving other persons. As concerning as this may be to many people, the individual temptations and failings are only the beginning root cause of the damage occurring within the overall church. The tragic reality we must all admit is this: the barrier of comparison has essentially now become embedded into the very fabric, the DNA, of most evangelical churches today!

Honestly, I'm not all that surprised. I'm deeply concerned, but not shocked by what's transpired! Allow me to explain.

Take a look around and it's not difficult to see that we've become a society of comparison. We've virtually become brainwashed by the barrage of media advertising to compare ourselves to others. How we look, how we dress, how we smell, the homes we live in, the cars we drive, the toys we have, the vacations we take, what we do for a living, how much money we make ... we exemplify consumer comparison at its worst.

This comparison mentality pervades well beyond an individual person's mind-set, as it's what drives most of our society today. Sports teams, books, CDs, DVDs, movie tickets, retail stores, vehicles, appliances, the top one hundred songs in America, vacation destinations, hotels, restaurants ... I could fill in pages, if not an entire book on the list of competitive corporate structures within our country. If it has any significance, if it can be measured or put into a viable descending order, you can bet it is compared and ranked accordingly.

Oh by the way, did I happen to mention worship service attendance? American evangelical churches (and others, for that matter) have several ranking sources that not only monitor but also publish their numbers. How many members, how many attend on an average weekend, how many locations or campuses ... it's all there. Compared and ranked for anyone who has the interest to discover the documented research!

It's no wonder why so many people arrive to the house of the Lord already in their established attitudes of self-comparison. Men checking out who drives what kind of car or truck, the year, make, model, perhaps a tow hitch for hauling a boat or RV ... women looking at what the other ladies are wearing, their hair, makeup, nails, and of course, jewelry. Come on now, let's be honest about this. I can't begin to number the various types of comparison conversations I've heard over the years. I'll bet you have as well! I can tell you in all honesty that more than a few times I was the instigator of this type of comparison discourse, and I'm not proud of that by any means.

Let's not attempt to fool ourselves with this, because we sure aren't pulling this over on God who sees our hearts and knows our thoughts. We need to admit that we can be cruel at times with our comparativeness toward others. Over the years, I've had pastor friends tell me of their having received written comments from the congregation, whereby their sermons were often critiqued, evaluated, graded, and sometimes compared to other preachers. Having known many vocalists, musicians, and worship leaders over the course of years, they too have told me of their having received such assessments.

Musical teams, choirs, pastors, and those in ministry alike, find themselves in this whole comparison arena. From the instruments they have, to the robes they wear, the way they get to dress, the size of the ministry, the pulpit they preach from ... this whole tragic comparison barrier is nothing new to our society or within the church. But I do believe it's becoming far more detrimental to our times of worship and as a result, has had a profound effect upon our vertical experience with God. When we arrive so immersed in comparing the horizontal, it's tough to transcend into an authentic vertical mind-set, the deliberate conscience focus upon God's glory.

> What is causing the quarrels and fights among you? Don't they come from the evil desires at war within you? You want what you don't have, so you scheme and kill to get it. You are jealous of what others have, but you can't get it, so you fight and wage war to take it away from them. Yet you don't have what you want because you don't ask God for it. And even when you ask, you don't get it because your motives are all wrong—you want only what will give you pleasure.
>
> (James 4:1–3 ESV)

Chapter 14

ENCUMBERED BY PRIDE AND EGO

When we truly seek to understand the foundational source of so many of these monstrous blockades, these stupendous stumbling blocks that stand in the way of our receiving much blessing, we need to look no further than two sources: pride and ego! Now, if I were standing across from you at this moment and was going to point an accusatory finger, I'd have to turn it upon myself. And that's precisely what I'm going to do here, in telling you of how God disclosed to me several years ago the issues of pride and ego, which I desperately needed to contend with in my own life.

Let me begin by telling you, this is one of those areas that God pointed out to me that needed much change, and what I needed to learn wasn't pleasant, not by any stretch of the imagination. Truth be told, it was downright painful! The damaging revelation of those two words pierced my soul! As sobering as that was, I pray what

God showed me back then never loses its impact. The message was loud and clear ... and my being deaf was no excuse not to listen. And you can bet that God made sure I didn't tune out!

Tim, Timmy, Timothy—pride and ego—your pride and ego are the true source of your comparison mentality. All the things in life that you line up, rank, evaluate, and compare ... all of the criteria in measuring your self-worth, your standing, your position—your, your, your ... me, me, me ... I, I, I—there it is, Tim, your triple-threat front and center. It's your pride and ego that are the most tragic obstacles you keep running into and the stumbling blocks you so easily fall over. Wow! I mean it was a real "in your face" revelation, one I couldn't ignore any longer.

The message cut deep, and I sure needed the *spiritual surgery*! Oh, let me tell you, no surgical operation is pleasant to go through, not at any time! Yet when life-threatening conditions call for them, you learn to focus beyond the temporal physical discomforts and center your thoughts upon the potential positive outcome. I know a great deal about this, as I've been through several major surgeries, including two brain-tumor operations. As challenging as those were, I must confess that I learned a couple of tremendous life lessons to apply metaphorically through those seasons and am blessed to have gone through those experiences.

You see the reality for me was that those tumors needed to be removed and the obstructions causing my impairments needed to be corrected. For me to have had ignored the warnings and medical advice of the doctors would have dramatically increased my mortality risk. To disregard their diagnosis and suggested course for remedy would've simply been both foolish and selfish on my part.

Yet, it was through those surgical adventures that I learned the valuable application that restoration and the process of healing can't begin until the damaging obstacles are removed! Not only does this hold truth for our physical well-being, it also applies to our spiritual health. For a believer to ignore the tumors of sin in their lives, in allowing them to grow, can bring about a spiritual death and most certainly mortify relationships. Sin, with its most treacherous tentacles that spread to destroy should be as paramount of concern to the Christian believer as physical cancerous tumors. It's imperative for us to comprehend that only through prayer, repentance, and removal of sinful actions will restoration and healing commence.

With steadfast assurance we can rest, knowing that no greater physician exists to heal the soul than Christ Jesus. With tender mercies, He most lovingly will come to our aid if we but seek Him to bring about a little spiritual surgery by the removing of the obstacles of sin and restore our spirits back to a rightful relationship with Him. I can testify that *spiritual surgery* now holds a new meaning with tremendous relevance for me: Christ is the great physician, the Holy Spirit is the surgeon, and prayer is the way I book the appointment.

Further, along that line of thinking, I've found it absolutely crucial for the recovery of any *spiritual surgery* to follow through with ongoing monitoring of the spiritual condition. For me, it's been essential to enlist the aid of a few trusted friends to help hold me accountable. And I can tell you unequivocally, there are rarely more sobering times than to have the right persons asking the right questions!

A recent reminder about *pride and ego*:

A longtime friend by the name of Don Moser, who's been a most trusted and treasured confidant for many years, sent me a little book to read. He told me how it had made a great impact upon his life, and he thought I might be challenged and blessed through reading this book. Well, let me tell you, once again I was confronted with a written message regarding the sins of "pride and ego" during my reading of *The Freedom of Self-Forgetfulness"* by Timothy Keller.[10]

Now, I'm going to be real candid here! The first time I read this book, I was frustrated and didn't like it much at all. It was too revealing, and I just wasn't ready to receive either its revelation or truthfulness. Truth be told, I was in a defensive mode while reading it, rather than seeking God to reveal truth. But then a few days later, I decided to take it into the sauna with me, thinking to myself, *Maybe I'll just peruse through it once more and see how it goes.* And so I read perhaps the first ten pages of this forty-seven-page book again. And then the next day a bit more, and a little more each day thereafter.

As I'm typing out this sentence, I would estimate I've now read through that book by Timothy Keller more than a dozen times. My first copy became so marked up and highlighted that I had to purchase another copy to start over in order to add more notes and new highlights. I want to keep it fresh and in-my-face relevant. I've asked my wife to hold me accountable to read through it at least once per month. I'm now passing it along to other men whom I consider dear brothers in Christ and asking them to hold me accountable as well.

Let me clarify that the previous paragraphs are not intended to be blown up as a type of written infomercial. It's me, openly confessing to you the reader that as a member of the church, the body of believers who are in Christ Jesus, I passionately and most desperately desire to arrive to the house of God with the right attitude, the right frame of mind, the right posture and position

---

10   Timothy Keller, *The Freedom of Self-Forgetfulness* (10Publishing, a division of 10ofThose: Leyland, England).

of heart, mind, and soul! I don't want one single thing to be of hindrance, not one barrier to exist in my life that would obstruct my ability to offer holy acceptable worship worthy unto the Lord God Almighty. And if it comes by means of my having to read words of strong medicine and ask others to hold me accountable, then so be it!

God's Word is clear regarding the self-sins of pride and ego. They were Satan's chief sins and the primary downfall of all mankind. It took many years, but I finally had to come to terms with the truth that my justification in using comparison as a tool for musical endeavors was diametrically in opposition to Christian living. I desperately needed to understand that my rationalizing comparison as a useful tool and being so engrained into my personality neither justified it nor negated the dangers thereof. I'm not to compare myself, my talents, gifts, ministry work, or anything else to anyone else. It's God who is my judge!

Now we need to park here at this point, because there's even more for us to uncover, a yet much deeper truth. You see pride and ego are but the beginning origin of our elevating imagery of self-worth and our entire comparison ideology. As those two obstinate sin-filled barriers rise up around us and blockade much within our lives, we must realize they're the manifestation of a much more serious sin, and that is the sin of coveting. Pride, ego, and the self-sins are all rooted deep within in the sin of coveting. From desiring to deserving, agendas to accolades, and enticements to entitlements ... every one of these branches spreading outward stems from the root of coveting.

"Oh, are you kidding me, are you serious?" That's the question I asked myself. I mean, I couldn't be a Christian, a follower of Christ, an authentic believer, having tremendous adoration for God and struggle with coveting ... could I? After all, that's one of the ten biggies—"Thou shalt not covet"! Could I really have fallen off into that sinful trap of coveting?

All right, so now I'm going to present a couple of questions for you to ponder.

Do you feel the sin of coveting should be viewed as any less serious today that it was when God first gave it to Moses within His list of the original Ten Commandments?

Do you believe there are a great number of people who at some level struggle with the whole *comparison and coveting* entrapping sins and need to confess it and turn from such bondage?

Perhaps, could you be numbered along with myself, as one who needs to keep constantly aware of the Devil's enticements of coveting and quickly turn in prayer to Christ for protection?

I hope to inspire you toward further examination relating to the spirit of self-sins, pride, ego, comparison, and coveting with this excerpt from A. W. Tozer:

> The tragic results of this spirit are all about us. Shallow lives, hollow religious philosophies, the preponderance of the element of fun in gospel meetings, the glorification of men, trust in religious externalities, quasi-religious fellowships, salesmanship methods, the mistaking of dynamic personality for the power of the Spirit: these and such as these are the symptoms of an evil disease, a deep and serious malady of the soul ... To be specific, the self-sins are these: self-righteousness, self-pity, self-confidence, self-sufficiency, self-admiration, self-love and a host of others like them. They dwell too deep within us and are too much a part of our natures to come to our attention

> till the light of God is focused upon them. The grosser manifestations of these sins, egotism, exhibitionism, self-promotion, are strangely tolerated in Christian leaders even in circles of impeccable orthodoxy.[11]

Perhaps the words you've just read have hit close to home for you and you're feeling a stirring within. If so, don't continue to stumble around. I earnestly hope you'll consider seeking out a few of your most trusted friends. Seek to become vulnerable through spiritual accountability and allow the Holy Spirit to do His work within your life.

> When pride comes, then comes disgrace, but with humility comes wisdom.
>
> (Proverbs 11:2 NIV)
>
> Seeing then that we have a great High Priest who has passed through the heavens, Jesus the Son of God, let us hold fast our confession. For we do not have a High Priest who cannot sympathize with our weaknesses, but was in all points tempted as we are, yet without sin. Let us therefore come boldly to the throne of grace, that we may obtain mercy and find grace to help in time of need.
>
> (Hebrews 4:14–16 NKJV)

---

11 A. W. Tozer, *The Pursuit of God* (public domain, 1948).

Is There Ambition in My Heart

Is there ambition in my heart? Search, gracious God, and see;
Or do I act a haughty part? Lord, I appeal to Thee.
I charge my thoughts, be humble still, And all my carriage mild,
Content, my Father, with Thy will, And quiet as a child.
The patient soul, the lowly mind, Shall have a large reward;
Let saints in sorrow lie resigned, And trust a faithful Lord.[12]

---

12   "Is There Ambition in My Heart," lyrics by Isaac Watts (1719).

Chapter 15

Who's In Charge? A Snag in Supremacy!

In looking at our present-day evangelical worship services, we find that they predominately consist of having a threefold ministry that includes prayer, praise, and preaching of God's Word.

Within our churches today, the vast majority have within their internal framework organizational charts. Similar to those of corporations, they delineate both the titles and responsibilities of the church staff. Typically, those leadership charts will detail the specific areas of ministry that the staff persons oversee and provide leadership. As churches have grown considerably in size from the early church days of meeting within the homes of believers and having only two forms of church leadership, the lists of responsibilities of today's ministries and titles have increased accordingly. Needless to say, the larger the church, the greater the number of those on staff ... and rightfully so. For the most part, we've certainly outgrown the original two-office pastoral paradigm of the early church.

However, from what I've observed, with all these organizational flow charts and their ensuing assigned responsibilities, I believe there's been an increasing loss of authentic leadership's rightful roles as Christ originally intended within His church.

If we were to further examine a typical church here in North America, we'd discover with few exceptions, that nearly all of the various denominations have a person on staff whose official position is that of worship leader. As a matter of fact, many churches now have more than one person with this title and responsibility either as a paid position or volunteer.

Several years ago, I was a worship leader for a very large Sunday school class consisting of nearly two hundred persons each week. At the time, the church had more than one campus and as a result had several worship teams divided among the campuses on a rotational schedule. It's very common for larger churches, which have multiple teams of musicians and vocalists, to often have several persons who lead and minister to the various age groups and specific demographic ministries.

Considering the aforementioned, I want to take us deep into yet another biblical truth. This is one that we should carefully consider, as many churches have now become misguided and often abuse the title, role, and rightful positional person of "worship leader." What I'm about to impart to you here comes as a result of my personal *life lessons learned* and direct observations in having visited several churches over the last decade.

Although I may have had at one time the title and responsibility of being a *worship leader,* I believe I would've brought far greater glory to God had I acknowledged the reality that I was merely to be a *worship facilitator*. The biblical truth is that amid any gathering of believers for the purpose of exalting God, there is but one leader of divine authority to lead and guide, and that is the Holy Spirit.

I can only look back and try to image the innumerable times I must have stifled the ministry of the Holy Spirit in being so absorbed in song lists and production. I confess that there were far more Sundays where I planned out the program than I prayed for God's presence. The same would be true during my early years as a Bible teacher. I was determined to teach the lesson I had studied and planned, that nothing was going to interfere. I would write out timelines and practice, so it all fit into a nice program. ... Oh my, how I wish I could hit the pause button on my life's DVD, put it in reverse mode, and edit those days from when I had such presuming arrogance to think I could lead anyone into God's Word or acceptable worship of Him apart from the leading and guiding of the Holy Spirit.

With total integrity, we must acknowledge how prevalent this type of preprogramming has become for nearly every aspect of our modern worship gatherings. Allow me to illustrate this to help further clarify what's transpiring. There's a significant difference between the minister of God's Word who approaches the pulpit, prepared and postured for the leading of the Holy Spirit, and that of the minister who is prepared, yet program determined.

The latter of these two preachers does so with watch in hand, the entire service having been mapped out, down to the minute; and like clockwork, the service will begin and end with all the specific details having been fulfilled. While the prior minister arrives to the pulpit in all preparedness to deliver the message, yet there is within him, a personal resolve to submit to the Holy Spirit's leading at all times. His continual prayer throughout the week was for God to manifest Himself that coming weekend. As the Holy Spirit leads throughout the service, the pastor is not only willing, but eager to scrap the outlined program and submit all authority to the Spirit's leading. Although I referenced this toward the preaching portion of ministry, this applies to the totality of any worship service, to the times of praise, prayer, and preaching!

Although some might be eager to point fingers toward the leadership within a local church or particular denomination for allowing this to occur, the overall body of believers would have to take equal responsibility. After all, how many of us would truly be okay attending a Sunday morning service beginning at 9:00 a.m. that continued on into the second service and went for four hours straight? Can you imagine, a four-hour or even perhaps a five-hour worship service, where God was so prevailing, touching the hearts and lives of people, that no one wanted to leave? It would be as if heaven itself had opened up and the glories of God were present. Can you fathom such a time of worship and being in the presence of God Almighty?

I never could before! How could I? I was too busy looking at my stupid outline, timeline, agenda, song lists, and all the other programmed materials. How could I possibly see God manifest Himself into my narrow-minded thinking or the lives of those around me, when I was so preoccupied with all that prearranged material? Does that mean I don't prepare my teaching notes these days? Absolutely not! But I can tell you, there's absolutely nothing of any value that I might teach, preach, or make known from my depths of my heart to reach the ears of those within the sound of my voice, without the Holy Spirit's involvement. The Holy Spirit is the most essential aspect of each gathering of believers, and He must be invited with our submissive resolve, to have full authority and control of the time.

This is not a new barrier within the church, by any means! Yet, we seem to be amiss in learning from some of the great preachers of the past. Consider this text from the observations of Andrew Murray:

> Many people speak of these things in the church around them, and do not see the least prospect of ever having the things changed. There is no prospect until there comes a radical change, until the Church of God begins to see that every sin in the believer comes from the flesh, from fleshly life amid our religious activities, from striving in self-effort to serve God. Until we learn to make confession, and until we begin to see that we must somehow or other let God's Spirit in power back to His Church, we must fail ... If it is our faith that God is going to have mercy on His Church in these last ages, it will be because the doctrine and the truth about the Holy Spirit will not only be studied, but sought after with a whole heart—and not only because that truth will be sought after, but because ministers and congregations will cry: "We have grieved God's Spirit. We have tried to be Christian churches with as little as possible of God's Spirit. We have not sought to be churches filled with the Holy Spirit." All the weakness in the Church is due to the refusal of the Church to obey its God.[13]

Further, I direct us to a most sobering observation by A. W. Tozer. We should give careful thought to the striking truthfulness of his words and the relevance they hold for many of our present-day churches:

---

[13] From *The Essential Works of Andrew Murray*, published by Barbour Publishing, Inc. Used by permission." Page 1112, 1113.

> If the Holy Spirit was withdrawn from the church today, 95 percent of what we do would go on and no one would know the difference. If the Holy Spirit had been withdrawn from the New Testament church, 95 percent of what they did would stop, and everybody would know the difference.[14]

It's only now, long after I became deaf and the resounding lessons learned are ringing forth as clear as a bell, that I can draw attention to these biblical truths to those who teach God's Word or worship through song and facilitate others. And it's also a word of truth for each of us, that at all times in our walk of faith, we must turn and submit to the Holy Spirit's working, be it in our times of prayer or praise ... allowing the Spirit of truth to lead and guide us.

Now more than ever, I'm convinced if we can allow ourselves to get beyond the watching of the clock in our times of worship and submit to the governing of the Holy Spirit to do His work, we will honor God to truly be in our midst and manifest His glory. If we can reposition our mind-sets from horizontal programming to God's vertical priorities, I believe the outbreak of revival within the church will transpire like no other time in our country's history.

---

14 Ibid.

Chapter 16

THE DISCIPLESHIP DRAWBACK

Now the Holy Spirit tells us clearly that in the last times some will turn away from the true faith; they will follow deceptive spirits and teachings that come from demons. These people are hypocrites and liars, and their consciences are dead.

(1 Timothy 4:1–2 NLT)

But know this, that in the last days perilous times will come: For men will be lovers of themselves, lovers of money, boasters, proud, blasphemers, disobedient to parents, unthankful, unholy, unloving, unforgiving, slanderers, without self-control, brutal, despisers of good, traitors, headstrong, haughty, lovers of pleasure rather than lovers of God, having a form of godliness but denying its power.

(2 Timothy 3:1–5 NKJV)

How much longer will the church, the Christian community, the body of believers in Christ continue to ignore the prophetic warnings so clearly defined in God's Word?

To what degree are we going to stand by with such apathy, willing to watch the multitudes of persons abandon their faith and walk away from the church?

To what extent will we continue to witness such staggering divorce rates among professed Christian homes, without grieving over the *death* of yet another ended marriage?

To what magnitude are we willing to endure the witness of so many lives suffering from brokenness of fellowship with God as they stammer through their beliefs, before we're provoked toward snatching those souls from the grip of the world?

One only needs to invest a few days of research in order to discover the reported epidemic numbers of people walking away from their faith and fellowship. At the time of this writing, I discovered several different sources stating between 3,500 to 4,000 churches close their doors each year, while approximately 4,000 to 4,500 churches are being planted. Conversely, other statistics record the opposite; they state that more churches are closing each year than are being planted.

Yet, even if the number of churches closing equaled the church plants, we would still have the stark reality of population growth within the United States. In order to meet the needs of our anticipated population by 2050 here in the United States, church-planting networks believe well over ten thousand churches need to be established each year in order to meet the demands of the anticipated population increase. More importantly, these church plants spoken of can't be looked upon with false assumptions in gaining ground, if all that is occurring is a mere shifting of bodies ... people moving from one congregation to another.

To compound the seriousness of this most alarming barrier, we can no longer ignore the number of believers who are walking away from their faith each day. In recent months, I was able to find several sources publishing the most alarming numbers, which quite literally grieved my soul. Some sources state the number at four thousand per day, while other sources listed that number at nearly six thousand. I ask you to consider conservatively a number of *four thousand* persons who at one time professed to be Christians, followers of Christ, are now walking away from the church every single day! That's nearly 1,500,000 people every year giving up, abandoning their corporate times of worship, prayer, and fellowship, and perhaps their faith entirely!

Their reasons for turning away and tuning out should be of no surprise for those who have active dialogue within the body of believers. All too common are the vexations from those who once so outwardly proclaimed God's praises, yet now so openly divulge their frustrations and skepticism. They've reached a tipping point in having too many hypocritical experiences, finding lots of religion and too few trusting relationships, having ongoing unanswered prayers, being exhausted from all of life's activities, and being hurt by other Christians.

When I consider the number of those who were once close personal friends, those who have lost their first love of God ... it's heartbreaking! Frequently, I'll genuinely struggle when watching those who at one time were passionate, dynamic, and fiery followers of Christ, but now are spiritually listless, dull, and indifferent.

Let's be honest about this and admit it, that the repercussions are most tragic and ever present. The consequences of consumerism within the church have brought about both shallow faith and underdeveloped knowledge of biblical doctrine. The lack of our holding one another biblically accountable for the purpose of edifying each other has resulted in the forgoing numbers of souls surrendering to the pressures of the world.

> The seeds on the rocky soil represent those who hear the message and receive it with joy. But since they don't have deep roots, they believe for a while, then they fall away when they face temptation.
>
> (Luke 8:13 NLT)
>
> Go therefore and make disciples of all the nations, baptizing them in the name of the Father and of the Son and of the Holy Spirit, teaching them to observe all things that I have commanded you.
>
> (Matthew 28:19–20 NKJV)

Christ's command was then and remains today explicitly clear: we're to "go make disciples," not just convert the community. Yet, that is precisely where the majority of evangelical churches suffer. There are lots of programs to reach the lost, community outreach activities like never before in our history, and yet, the highest primary goal of ministry should be to "go make disciples." However, in many churches, it is all but nonexistent.

Of the evangelical communities that do offer some type of discipleship program, it's more geared toward a "discipleship in a box" program, rather than an ongoing committed investment by the church leadership. Christ invested three years of His life into a core group of twelve men. Three years of His life! Virtually seven days per week, He ministered, instructed, and helped established their faith! And that, my friends, is exemplified biblical equipping, the authority in example of authentic discipleship!

Today, most churches that offer any sort of discipleship training somehow think they can accomplish something viable one day per week for six to eight weeks. This begs the question, "So how's that working out for us these days?"

If we look at the first commandment given to us by Christ in the New Testament as found in Matthew 22:37–39, we find no margin for latitude toward individual interpretation: "And he said to him, 'You shall love the Lord your God with all your heart and with all your soul and with all your mind. This is the great and first commandment. And a second is like it: You shall love your neighbor as yourself.'"[15] As these are the first and foremost two commandments, we find no less of command from Christ in His last charge to us:

> Go therefore and make disciples of all nations, baptizing them in the name of the Father and of the Son and of the Holy Spirit, teaching them to observe all that I have commanded you.
>
> (Matthew 28:19–20 ESV)

There has never been a time since Jesus spoke these words, whereby He permitted us to have liberty or discretionary choosing of which commands to obey or ignore.

Andrew Murray's words echo down the corridor of time, in providing the following powerful message toward our charge in following Christ's great command and commission unto us:

> The command is no arbitrary law from outside. It is simply the revelation, for our intelligent and

---

15 ESV

voluntary consent, of the wonderful truth that we are His body, that we now occupy His place on earth, and that His will and love now carry out through us the work He began, and that now in His place we live to seek the Father's glory in winning a lost world back to Him.[16]

I've become exceeding passionate toward the revival of authentic discipleship! This can only come about through commitment of church leadership willing to invest in the lives of those who desire to follow Christ as genuine disciples. And it's those whom we make disciples, who in turn, will most likely desire themselves to "go make disciples." Yet, until Christian leadership accepts the responsibility and takes Christ's command seriously, the graphic and tragic truth is there will be an increase in the numbers of those who will walk away from the faith.

This was the last chapter in my writing of this book. At first, I questioned the topic of discipleship being brought into the scope of worship and perhaps it might have served better if it was left for a future publication. However, within a few days of deliberating on this notion, with crystal clear conviction I recognized that nothing could be more paramount for us to get our heads around!

How can we possibly expect believers to mature into Christlikeness, become steadfast in their faith, equipped to worship God in spirit and truth, apart from the committed long-term investment of discipleship?

Would we dare to think that perhaps Christ didn't know what was the absolute best for becoming authentic worshippers of Him? Of course not! The significance of the repercussions in

---

16 From *The Essential Works of Andrew Murray*, published by Barbour Publishing, Inc. Used by permission." Page 733.

not following the Great Commission, in of itself, is the church's collective apostasy (rebellion) in not obeying Christ's command.

> But the end of all things is at hand; therefore be serious and watchful in your prayers. And above all things have fervent love for one another, for "love will cover a multitude of sins." Be hospitable to one another without grumbling. As each one has received a gift, minister it to one another, as good stewards of the manifold grace of God.
>
> (1 Peter 4:7–10 NKJV)
>
> Now to him who is able to keep you from stumbling and to present you blameless before the presence of his glory with great joy, to the only God, our Savior, through Jesus Christ our Lord, be glory, majesty, dominion, and authority, before all time and now and forever. Amen.
>
> (Jude 24–25 ESV)

Chapter 17

Preventing Presence While Promoting Programs

> It is in the process of being worshipped that God communicates His presences to men.
>
> —C. S. Lewis

How often do we allow ourselves to become so preoccupied with programs and activities for God that we lose sight of the presence and adoration of God? We think God is pleased by all of our busyness and service for Him, but God is far more concerned about our brokenness in humility and selflessness in our lives of worshipful living. I believe there are a great number of churches that have literally buried themselves in works of community outreach, building campaigns, and micro-ministry programs, such as; fishing, bowling, knitting, and their seemingly endless multitude of felt-needs ministries.

Most commonly found within these sprawling ministerial churches are two groups of people. The first being those who have literally become exhausted as a result of all of their undertakings. While their talents are being used in service, their inability to maintain a healthy balance of God, family, work, and church has all but been siphoned. The physical tiredness from their overcommitting eventually takes its toll. Many who once had such a fervent fire within are now left smoldering, having been burned out.

Then there's the second group of folks who have virtually unending energies and thrive from all of the engagements of their works. Their entire focus is upon those of the minor and micro-ministry programs, while they direct little attention toward the major three biblical commands of worship, prayer, and study of God's Word. Quick to volunteer, they're frequently placed into various leadership roles and charged with the associated ministry functionalities. Yet, many of these same persons could never handle such similar responsibilities within the secular workforce. Rushed into leadership and having minimal accountability, the Enemy is able to focus on those not fully equipped, attacking on all fronts with the temptations of pride, self-worth, self-promotion, and sanctimonious stature.

True are the words of Roy Hession as he observed so rightly the end results of many who confuse the work of ministerial service:

> If we are making service for Him and end in itself we will be full of reactions and will want to fight back or to break away and start an independent work of our own, and we become more self-centered than ever.[17]

---

17 Roy and Revel Hession, *We Would See Jesus* (CLC Publications: Fort Washington, PA.), 24. Used by permission.

Within these same two groups of people, we find the pendulum moving from those who are battered from the waves of imbalance and self-exertion, to those having great self-expectation, yet who are unequipped and often spiritually immature.

If you think I'm being a bit harsh here, I'd strongly encourage you to look around! Ask God to open the eyes of your understanding and reveal just how far the Devil has infiltrated many of these types of church-supported ministries.

From home groups to small groups, Bible studies, worship teams, choirs, and effectively every ministry within the church, all too common are the evidences of gossip, jealousy, resentment, and social click segregation. These divisive attitudes and activities are running rapid throughout the church, fanned by the Enemy's desire to undermine the work we do for the glory of God.

While we attempt to mask the realities of these occurrences and diminish the potency of the venom, not for a single moment should we consider that God doesn't see the totality of the situation. From the actions of our hands to the attitudes of our hearts, God knows and sees it all!

I know all too well about the attacks and schemes of the Enemy in such ministries. I've experienced firsthand the painful realities while in leadership and confess my own weaknesses, temptations, and failings in the past. I'm ashamed to admit that I've been a part of the gossip chain and perhaps have added links to it. I've had times of being filled with jealousy and scorching moments of resentment and gravitating toward specific socially prominent groups in trying to improve my stature in service.

Let me stop and be absolutely clear here that in no way am I trying to communicate that ministry activities or programs based upon biblical mandates are invalid, harmful, or damaging within themselves. However, we must acknowledge the ever-present dangers as a result of the personal temptations for people to start and head up every sort of felt-needs ministry.

Look where we're at today. We have a profusion of programs in most every area within the church. Hands of volunteers seemingly rise up faster than ministries can be implemented or managed. But just because a ministry seems imaginable on paper doesn't mean it's automatically manageable by people.

I remember many years ago hearing someone say, "If the Devil can't make you bad, he'll make you busy." There is some truth to that statement right there.

> Be still, and know that I am God! I will be honored by every nation. I will be honored throughout the world.
>
> (Psalm 46:10 NLT)

Chapter 18

The Blockade of Busyness

The entire barricade of busyness, the chaotic and hectic pace in which we live our lives in this age, would have been unthinkable fifty years ago. The overabundance of activities with which we can occupy ourselves these days to fill our voids are virtually innumerable. From one stimulation to another and with a vastness of modalities from physical outdoor activities to armchair 3-D gaming, we can engross ourselves from the moment we open our eyes in the morning until we close them at night in utter exhaustion.

The overindulgence of busyness within every moment of life has sadly hindered much in the way of many a believer's individual spiritual growth. Our society moves at a rapid tempo from event to event, with little or no time to meet with God in the moments. All too frequently are the exclusive responses of "I've got too much going on this week to make Bible study," "Didn't have time to read the Word," "Haven't done morning devotionals in months, I'm just way too busy," "Don't go to church, because I just don't have the time."

I mean to tell you, I've heard just about all the "busy" reasons you can comprehend, and no doubt had a few of my own over the years. I would ask you to think about when the last time your personal devotion of studying God's Word canceled out your most pressing scheduled appointment or activity. It sure appears that everything else takes priority these days ... doesn't it?

Perhaps you're sensing at this point just how serious of an obstruction this barrier has become toward our ability to live continually in communion with God. We can't be shadowboxing around this—it's way too serious for us to ignore! If we truly look at the monumental impact of the busyness barrier, it's "damming"! We're talking massive stopping power that holds back the flow of the mightiest rivers of blessing ... that kind of damming. What's more, God only knows (literally) the impact all this busyness has brought about in the lives of countless numbers of people, blockading their spiritual walk of faith and love for God ... and that is a whole different kind of damning.

I hope to encourage you here to think about the aspects of worshipping in spirit and truth. God knows our schedules! He created the concept of time! Our being too busy not to praise, pray, or participate in fellowship doesn't hold any validity with Him. I firmly believe this is an area we need to just get right with God and confess our being overly and overtly busy. Read the following quote a few times and give it careful consideration. Because, if we examine the reality of what Chuck Swindoll once stated, then we'll be forced to accept the truth of it and hopefully be inspired to make a change:

> We are often so caught up in our activities that we tend to worship our work, work at our play, and play at our worship.

If we can get this in check, reprioritize what matters most in life, and have it reflected in our daily activities, we'll soon find ourselves being able to be openly truthful in our relationship with God. Once we're in that right posture of truthfulness, where our attitudes and actions match, we'll begin to experience the sweetness of fellowship again. When we get into that internal posture spiritually, we can then move outwardly toward authentic fellowship with one another. Then and only then, will we be able to speak the truth in love to each other, encourage, forgive, and build up one another for the sake of the edification of the body of believers.

> Come to Me, all you who labor and are heavy laden, and I will give you rest. Take My yoke upon you and learn from Me, for I am gentle and lowly in heart, and you will find rest for your souls.
>
> (Matthew 11:28–29 NKJV)

Within the two verses above, we discover two times Jesus promised us *rest*. Jesus promises to give us rest, and we will find rest for our souls if we but come to Him.

So let me ask you, Are you finding rest for your soul?

Chapter 19

COMPROMISING: A DETOUR FROM COMMITMENT

In a culture virtually filled with *compromise*, the ideology of *commitment* now seems to be a foreign concept. The compass of moral righteousness is no longer pointing toward Christ and has no predetermined set course. For those persons who truly seek being purposed toward a life marked by commitment, it will mandate utter resolve to forgo the social appeals of middle-ground mindsets. It will require our most earnest commitment and diligent practice in order to live holy and worshipful lives unto the Lord.

I view the discipline of commitment as a lifelong journey and not as a destination. I will never arrive at a highest point in my relationship with God or worship of Him until I'm at home in heaven. It's not like I'm going to one day be able to state, "I've reached the apex of commitment, the ultimate pinnacle." Commitment isn't something one achieves! It's steadfast faithfulness exemplified over the course of an entire lifetime. Those individuals who most exemplify faithful commitment will most likely not receive the highest forms of recognition until after they're no longer living. It will be through their life's example, which so greatly influenced other people, whereby those who were so richly impacted will testify of that person's steadfast endurance, devotion, and committed faithfulness.

Being predetermined to be utterly devout, unwaveringly faithful, and passionate in our relationship to God is not going to be without significant challenges. Satan is always on the prowl, ready to take aim at our moments of weakness, resolved to "zero in" on the defining targets of our various temptations. Those who follow the ways of the world carry with them an abundance of the ammunition of compromise. They're quick to sight the target and fire at will toward any who would voice a strong opposition to sin, apathy, or appeasement toward God's Word.

Once again, I remind us that having an attitude of "it's all good" is not a worthy practice for the believer in Christ. In point of fact, it's unbiblical! Sin will never be good nor will God ever compromise His position toward sin. The "coexist" and "it's all good" philosophies have merely transformed the minds of those who accept such beliefs to that of indifference and a branding of "let's compromise"! Consider the words of J. Vernon McGee as he wrote about the compromising of sin within the church:

> There are many people today who want to argue religion, but they don't want to live it. I'm convinced that most of the superficiality in our churches today is there as a cover-up of sin. Unfortunately our churches our honeycombed with hypocrisy, a compromise with evil, and a refusal to face up to sin. You know, it's easy to preach about the sin of

the Moabites which they committed about 4,000 years ago, but what about our sins today? It was the brother of Henry Ward Beecher who said, "I like a sermon where one man is the preacher and one man is the congregation so that when the preacher says, 'Though art the man,' there's no mistaking whom he's talking about."[18]

It's certainly taken me a long time to learn about the differences between my commitment to God and His commitment to me. For many years, I was perplexed with a false theology in understanding God's unfailing and unwavering commitment to me. Often, I felt as though my emotional feelings were based upon God's love for me, and I equated my ups and downs in life with God's position of nearness to my life. I had to learn that good days of emotional highs don't equate with God being any nearer than the days I'm in a funk and struggling with depression. My frame of mind has no impact on God's faithfulness.

I constantly need to be mindful that He remains faithful and true in His covenant relationship with me, even when I'm not moving toward Him. He continually dwells within me and there is no time He is not! The Holy Spirit of God has taken up residence in my soul, and although I may do things that quench the Spirit's working within my life, nothing will ever cause Him to depart. Simply put, God is with me at all times, in woe and in well. That's powerful right there!

In woe and well … It's hard for most people to contemplate embracing the seasons of woe. We all like the times of being well, but the woes are often the precursors to the wells of life. Oswald Chambers said it this way:

---

18   J. Vernon McGee, *Thru the Bible*, volume 4, 390.

> The agony of man's affliction is often necessary to put him into the right mood to face the fundamental things of life. The psalmist says, "Before I was afflicted I went astray; but now I have kept Thy Word."[19]

It's imperative for us to understand that no matter what circumstances we face—our testing, trials, or temptations—God's faithfulness and commitment to us never falters nor diminishes. He has entered into a covenant relationship with us through our confession of Christ Jesus, His Son, and He cannot go back on His promises.

That said, we must recognize that depending on our freewill choices in this life and our responses to various circumstances, we might very well do certain things that grieve the Holy Spirit and hinder our relationship with God. We may distance ourselves as a result of our sins, refusing to allow spiritual conviction to prompt us to confess and turn from those behaviors, but God will never move away or move out from His dwelling within the lives of His children.

Barriers may surround us at times, overshadow and obstruct all sorts of the intentional *good works* we're so busy about, but God is forever unfailing in His commitment to us. It's never too late and the barriers will never become so big that God isn't able to remove them and bring forth restoration and revival. We can take great confidence in that truth, finding rest and assurance of hope!

I wholeheartedly believe the church of today needs to take a stand. It's time to draw a line and expel the cultural precepts of compromise, tolerance, and appeasement in seeking the approval of the masses, as this neither equips the saints nor glorifies God. God is seeking the hearts of those willing to worship Him in spirit

---

19   Oswald Chambers (1874–1917).

and truth. He longs for our adoration and commitment, not all of our activities and commotion. God is calling us to be still, to know Him, to hear from Him, and to experience Him in authentic intimacy.

Think of what would happen if we gathered together with the sole intent of truly seeking to glorify God. Where we no longer sought to be entertained or amused through secularities, trendy commodities, or cultural compromise for the sake of worldly appeal. Imagine the power unleashed through the working of the Holy Spirit within the individual lives of those attending as we submit to His authority and leading. Let us envision the blessing that would fall upon us as we purposed to gaze upon the glories of Christ, with our every intent to live as worthy worshippers of the Lord God Almighty!

> But you must remember, beloved, the predictions of the apostles of our Lord Jesus Christ. They said to you, "In the last time there will be scoffers, following their own ungodly passions." It is these who cause divisions, worldly people, devoid of the Spirit. But you, beloved, building yourselves up in your most holy faith and praying in the Holy Spirit, keep yourselves in the love of God, waiting for the mercy of our Lord Jesus Christ that leads to eternal life.
>
> (Jude 17–21 ESV)

Section 3

A Journey Beyond the Barriers

Chapter 20

A Shift Toward Worshipping in Spirit and Truth

When we want to look to the basic foundation of how we're to glorify, exalt, and honor God, we only need to look at the words Christ spoke on the subject. His message was direct—to the point and profound! And if we truly desire to get back to the heartfelt foundation of glorifying the Lord and invite the manifold presence of God to meet us each week, then we must follow the teaching of Christ as found in the fourth chapter of John's gospel.

During His conversation with a Samaritan woman at Jacob's well, the woman questioned Jesus about where and how she was to worship God. In His reply, Jesus was clear: God is seeking persons who will worship Him in spirit and in truth.

> You worship what you do not know; we know what we worship, for salvation is of the Jews. But

the hour is coming, and now is, when the true worshipers will worship the Father in spirit and truth; for the Father is seeking such to worship Him. God is Spirit, and those who worship Him must worship in spirit and truth.

(John 4:22–24 NKJV)

Notice that Christ didn't provide an answer with "multiple choices" or give us the leeway and various options to worship Him how we might see fit. There is a core foundation consisting of two essential elements toward the genuine worship of God to be discovered within Christ's response.

The first is that we must worship God in *spirit*. Notice, Jesus didn't say we would worship in the Holy Spirit. The transliteration implicitly refers to *the spirit*, that is, our internal human spirit, our innermost being. By these words, we understand it to mean within the core fabric of our very souls and all that is within us, we're to give glory and honor to God. From an outpouring of our souls, overflowing with adoration to God, this is what truly defines the core essence of how to worship in *spirit*.

Secondly, we must worship God in *truth*. God is seeking the authenticity of our hearts, pouring out with genuine praise and our expressions of love to Him. We're to worship wholeheartedly and with unreserved truthfulness.

These two essential elements toward our being able to worship in spirit and truth are but the beginning of our responsibility for holy worship. If we were to stop right with Jesus' instruction to the Samaritan woman, we would miss out on a critical truth of biblical doctrine. What Jesus said to her applied to those people prior to Him going to the cross, His resurrection, ascension, and Pentecost. In her question to Jesus, the woman wanted to know where she should go to worship and perhaps confess her sins. And in His reply, Jesus explained to her that the time was soon coming where neither the Samaritan temple or the Jewish temple or synagogues were going to be the places one would have to seek forgiveness or assemble to worship God.

Pentecost was the beginning of the New Testament church, and with the arrival and indwelling work of the Holy Spirit, a new aspect of the holy worship of God was manifest. Through genuine conversion and regeneration of one's life, the Christian believer's authentic glorification of God is evidenced, whereby he or she worships from the total internal being, in all truth, humility, reverence, and wholehearted adoration of the triune God. In addition to the Holy Spirit taking up permanent residence in the life of each believer, there's the work of His external activities as we gather together with other Christians.

The Holy Spirit is in fact, the Spirit of truth, who intercedes on our behalf through Christ Jesus and to the Father in totality of truth in all His workings. God cannot lie, and no part of God can receive anything less than that which is offered in truth. We worship in *spirit and truth*, through the power and workings of the Holy Spirit of truth! Therefore, for us to worship in spirit and truth, we desperately need the Holy Spirit convicting us of any false ideologies, deceptive doctrines of spoken word or lyrics sung, anything whereby the ignorance of our actions would become a barrier to our worshipping in all truth.

Let's look back at John 4:24 one more time here, as there's yet another essential lesson for us to learn:

> God is spirit, and those who worship him must worship in spirit and truth.
>
> (John 4:24 ESV)

"God is spirit." This is paramount, at the apex of our much-needed apprehension! God is neither bound by space or time as nothing can contain Him. Therefore, He's not limited to sanctuaries, temples, churches, basilicas, or any building created by man. His presence, in being omnipresent, is one of the attributes so often forgotten by many believers. They fail to realize that when it comes to worship, they don't need to wait to be in a building of any sort or with any particular group of people.

Commenting on this verse of John 4:24, Andrew Murray, in his book *The School of Obedience*, calls to our attention the desperate need for Christians to understand the depth of what it means to worship God in spirit and truth.

> A lesson of deep importance: How much of our Christianity suffers from this—that it is confined to certain times and places. A man who seeks to pray earnestly in the church or in the closet spends the greater part of the week or the day in a spirit entirely at odds with that in which he prayed. His worship was the work of a fixed place or hour, not of his whole being. God is a Spirit: He is the everlasting and unchangeable One. What He is, He is always and in truth. Our worship must likewise be in spirit and truth: His worship must be the spirit of our life and our life must be the worship in spirit as God is Spirit.[20]

There is much for us to learn in becoming worshippers whom God seeks. But learning all the truth one could glean of this single biblical lesson is of no value whatsoever without practicing that which God requires of us.

---

[20] From *The Essential Works of Andrew Murray*, published by Barbour Publishing, Inc. Used by permission." Page 753.

For you were once darkness, but now you are light in the Lord. Walk as children of light (for the fruit of the Spirit is in all goodness, righteousness, and truth), finding out what is acceptable to the Lord.

(Ephesians 5:8–10 NKJV)

But God has revealed them to us through His Spirit. For the Spirit searches all things, yes, the deep things of God. For what man knows the things of a man except the spirit of the man which is in him? Even so no one knows the things of God except the Spirit of God.

(1 Corinthians 2:10–11 NKJV)

Chapter 21

Returning to Christ

Returning to Christ! The words are so easily read, yet they are so powerfully a challenge to many who profess to follow Him each day. It's not a matter of claiming to believe in Christ; it's a matter of allowing Him to be above all and in all we do, for Him to have lordship of our lives, for His glory alone. To return to Christ and to have Him at the epicenter of our lives requires the renewal of our thinking of Christ. Having an incorrect understanding of Christ will never lead a believer to possessing a right relationship with Him.

Through careful and deliberate rightful contemplation of God (the deity of the triune God, the Godhead), we must remember that in Christ Jesus, all things were created by Him and for Him. Let's pause a moment and look at the biblical truth discovered in the first chapter from the book of Colossians: *All things were created by Him and for Him in heaven and on earth.* "All things"—not some things or a number of things ... all things!

Our returning to Christ in desiring for Him to have sole position and soul possession upon the throne of our hearts should lead us to careful thought of our connectivity to God. We have to understand that along with creating us in the image of God, came the uniqueness of our soul. No other created creature by God possesses the soul. We were designed and designated to be united with Him in constant fellowship. The trinity of God in all power, wisdom, and goodness blessed His created image, bearing His likeness, and therefore, rejoices unceasingly in that which He created. God saw before the creation of the world, before the foundations were laid and from without beginning, the souls in each of us, those who would please, glorify, and worship Him without end. How amazing and awesome for us to embrace this truth!

We must never forget that God loves, protects, and guides that which Christ created. Unceasingly rejoicing and taking divine pleasure in us, we are the affection of His creation! Let us never lose sight or understanding that God loved us before we came into being, and we love Him now because He first loved us! He glories in us, the bride of Christ! He longs for our intimate fellowship, through the giving of our time, devotion, and adoration to Him! As we do, He receives those actions of love from us, His children, whom He cherishes without measure and without end.

Our Confidence in Christ

You know, sometimes we can read through specific passages of the Bible numerous times and suddenly, a new truth previously unrealized will be discovered. That's one of the great aspects of studying God's Word. There's always more for us to uncover, more to seek out and apply to our lives. We must never forget that ongoing study of God's Word, deliberate reading, and prayerful meditation is the best way for us to know Him. The more we invest in seeking true understanding of who God is as He is revealed to us through His written Word, the greater clarity and correct understanding we'll have.

Allow me to recount one such example that was uncovered through prayerful study of the following verses. I never grasped the imagery here before, but as the barriers within my life began to be chipped away, God was ever faithful to reveal the things I missed prior to that time. These verses portray a glorious vision of Christ and have led me to a much greater understanding of a tremendous truth. I hope you'll take note here of this most powerful reminder of Christ's position in returning to Him.

> In the year that King Uzziah died, I saw the Lord sitting on a throne, high and lifted up, and the train of His robe filled the temple.
>
> (Isaiah 6:1 NKJV)
>
> I watched till thrones were put in place, And the Ancient of Days was seated; His garment was white as snow, And the hair of His head was like pure wool. His throne was a fiery flame, Its wheels a burning fire.
>
> (Daniel 7:9 NKJV)
>
> ... According to the working of His mighty power which He worked in Christ when He raised Him from the dead and seated Him at His right hand in the heavenly places.
>
> (Ephesians 1:19–20 NKJV)

If you read through the above passages again, you'll notice that Christ is seated. He is not moving about or busy tending to this or that. His position is clearly stated by Isaiah, Daniel, and Paul.

Christ is seated upon the throne. When we contemplate Christ's posture, Him being seated, we can take confidence that He is at His rightful place of righteousness and ruling. Being seated reveals one who is steadfast, secure, and at rest. All things are under His control. Nothing transpires without Him knowing it and allowing it to happen. Fully secure, fully at rest, fully in righteousness and ruling ... Christ Jesus sits upon the throne and watches over that which He created.

Chapter 22

BENEATH THE CROSS OF CHRIST JESUS

In our returning to Christ, we must not lose sight of Christ upon the cross. His work here on earth; the imputation of our sins, which He took upon Himself; and His substitutionary death for the atonement of our due penalty can never be viewed apart from the cross. Upon the cross, Christ Jesus paid the ultimate price and completed the work God the Father sent Him to do. For we who were neither worthy or ever could repay such a debt, our lives should reflect the upmost reverence and sincere love to our gracious, loving, and merciful Father.

I truly love these words of Alexander MacLaren! Even one hundred years after his death, we can learn much from his proclamation:

> The cross is the center of the world's history; the incarnation of Christ and the crucifixion of our Lord are the pivot round which all the events of the ages revolve. The testimony of Christ was the spirit of prophecy, and the growing power of Jesus is the spirit of history.[21]

R. A. Torrey, in his amazing message entitled "The Great Attraction—The Uplifted Christ,"[22] ever so eloquently reminds us of the power in which Christ Jesus draws the heart and soul:

> It is Christ crucified who draws; it is Christ crucified who meets the deepest needs of the heart of all mankind. It is an atoning Savior, a Savior who atones for the sins of men by His death, and thus saves from the holy wrath of an infinitely holy God, who meets the needs of men, and thus draws all men, for all men are sinners. Preach any Christ but a crucified Christ, and you will not draw men for long. Preach any gospel but a gospel of atoning blood, and it will not draw for long ... A theology without a crucified Savior, without the atoning blood, won't draw. It does not meet the need. No, no, the words of our Lord are still true, "And I, if I be lifted up from the earth, will draw all men unto myself."

Torrey continued with clarifying the meaning of John 12:32 as Jesus spoke to the people gathered around Him:

> "And I, if lifted up from the earth, will draw all peoples to myself ..." He did not say that He would draw every individual, but that all races of men: Greeks as well as Jews, Romans, Scythians,

---

21 Alexander MacLaren (1826–1910).

22 R. A. Torrey, "The Great Attraction," (1856–1928).

French, English, Germans, Japanese, Americans, and men of all nations. He is a universal Savior, and true Christianity is a universal religion. Mohammedanism, Buddhism, Confucianism, and all other religions, but Christianity, are religions of a restricted application. Christianity, with a crucified Christ as its center, is a universal religion that meets the needs of all mankind.[23]

Before the cross is where the heart of worship begins. It's there we find ourselves looking up unto Jesus, taking in what He did for us from completely unselfish love. Before the cross, we might stand with a heart filled with humility, and yet we would be driven to our knees with upmost gratitude in having a Savior who would take upon Himself our sins, our guilt, and our punishment all for love's sake. We will be restored and reunited with Him for we are His bride, His love, His glory and joy!

And yet it is the cross of Christ that I've discovered ever more frequently, which seems to be absent from within the buildings where so many Christians gather today. Many of the contemporary venues of worship in all their illustrious décor, sophisticated lighting, and elaborate sound systems, seem to have no room for the cross. Oh, they may have them in the foyer or creatively within the artwork of their signage, but how often is the cross absent at the center of the sanctuary. Nothing will bring the soul to the place and position of proper worship than to stand before the cross.

When standing with voices raised in worship, is there a cross to look upon to remind us of what should be our reverent posture before Christ? Amid the fashionable and esthetically enhanced decorum, is there a cross for us to draw our attention and quiet our souls? Perhaps the image of Christ on the cross has become too solemn for us to gaze upon with humility and integrity. It

---

23   Ibid.

might be that for many who attend, even the empty cross is just too confronting and convicting, reminding them of their need of a Savior. Perhaps the thought of Christ dying on the cross and giving up His life for their sins is just too sobering.

Too great a price was paid for us to be timid or un-embracing of all that Christ did for us upon the cross. For us to be without the cross in our places of worship, front and center to bring us to our knees within our hearts, minds, and souls, is to abstain from the foundation of worshipping in spirit and truth. Without the cross, we put ourselves at risk of becoming cross-less Christians. I believe there is nothing more important for a body of believers to look upon when gathering together to bring glory to God, than the cross itself. It's there that so often the nails of the cross penetrate our souls and allow us to come face-to-face with the King of Kings and Lord of Lords.

Beneath the Cross of Jesus

Beneath the cross of Jesus I fain would take my stand,
The shadow of a mighty rock within a weary land;
A home within the wilderness, a rest upon the way,
From the burning of the noontide heat, and the burden of the day.

Upon that cross of Jesus mine eye at times can see
The very dying form of One Who suffered there for me;
And from my stricken heart with tears two wonders I confess;
The wonders of redeeming love and my unworthiness.

I take, O cross, thy shadow for my abiding place;
I ask no other sunshine than the sunshine of His face;
Content to let the world go by to know no gain or loss,
My sinful self my only shame, my glory all the cross.[24]

---

24 "Beneath the Cross of Jesus," words by Elizabeth Cecelia Clephane (1872).

Chapter 23

Christ's Positional Preeminence

Now more than ever, I believe it's of paramount importance that we acknowledge Christ's preeminence as the head of His church. It's high time we get ourselves in the right position, an acceptable posture of the heart to bring about restoration and revival.

> Christ is the visible image of the invisible God. He existed before anything was created and is supreme over all creation, for through him God created everything in the heavenly realms and on earth. He made the things we can see and the things we can't see—such as thrones, kingdoms, rulers, and authorities in the unseen world. Everything was created through him and for him. He existed before anything else, and holds all

creation together. Christ is also the head of the church, which is his body.

(Colossians 1:15–18 NLT)

For years, I've been observing a significant number of professed Christians who have become very disillusioned, strolling along in life without realizing they are imminently close to spiritual death. The entertainment of the programs has lost its draw and many of these same people have made known to me that they're tired and bored with the whole church experience. They no longer crave God's Word nor consider it an honor or blessing to gather with other Christians to study God's Word or participate in corporate times of worship.

As a community of believers, perhaps we should give careful consideration to the following words of Duncan Campbell[25]:

> There is a growing conviction everywhere, and especially among thoughtful people, that unless revival comes, other forces will take the field, that will sink us still deeper into the mire of humanism and materialism.

Julian of Norwich in her book *Revelations of Divine Love*[26] detailed the words she received from Christ. In a most beautiful passage, she described the preeminence of Christ. In having read through this book several times, each time I come to this section of text, I find myself drawn into the person of Christ. Being reminded in all biblical truth that Christ is the one whom is to be most exalted. It is Christ whom I love, adore, and worship. It is Christ whom I

---

25 Duncan Campbell (1898–1972).
26 The Order of Julian of Norwich, *Revelations of Divine Love* (Paraclete Press, 2011).

serve. It is Christ whom I desire, yearn for, and long to be in His eternal presence. It is Christ whom I must preach and teach to those who are lost and in such desperate need of a Savior. In all things, Christ is preeminent!

Chapter 24

No Sidestepping Sin or Moving from Grace

It sure seems for the most part, the word *sin* has lost its sting of potency. In times past, Christian believers would've dared to contemplate the sinful activities that now are so blatantly acceptable within many of Christian circles. What at one time would've been unapologetically "called out" as actions in rebellion against God, are now most delicately approached with uttermost sensitivity and with careful attention toward not offending the other person.

Sin: although this three-letter word is singular in syllable, it is plural by nature in recourse. Sin never affects just one person. The repercussions ripple outward, with the end results often never fully realized. Few and far between are the Christian men and women who lament and grieve over their habitual sins, with a desire to repent and return to living for God in holy reverence.

The message of God's grace has covered so much of sin in our modern-day theology, that for many a nonbeliever, the lines of grace have been blurred until even those who know not Christ as Savior are persuaded that God's love and grace is sufficient enough to cover even the unrepentant.

Most people don't want to view the actions of sin under sin's true meaning. For the essence of sin signifies the actions of a person being in absolute opposition toward God's holiness and righteousness. Sin is a perversion of God's truth. Sin plagues the soul of mankind and spreads like a contagion, inflicting pain, suffering, and distress to all it attacks. At its core, sin is a purposeful violation against God's perfect and holy will for our lives. It is the highest form of treason unto God's kingdom, and no such betrayal can ever be allowed in heaven.

In the Bible, we discover that James in his letter to Christian believers detailed the methodology of sin, depicting how Satan works his plan of deception. From James' account of the Devil's progressive enticement, there's a paramount principle we need to learn: the Devil works ever so hard to lead believers into the areas of sin where they're most unwatchful. The cunning and planning of the Enemy lurks to challenge the lethargy of the unguarded, and when fully engaged, it can result in the most damaging of circumstances, even spiritual death.

> But each one is tempted when he is drawn away by his own desires and enticed. Then, when desire has conceived, it gives birth to sin; and sin, when it is full-grown, brings forth death. Do not be deceived, my beloved brethren.
>
> (James 1:14–16 NKJV)
>
> Stay alert! Watch out for your great enemy, the devil. He prowls around like a roaring lion, looking

for someone to devour. Stand firm against him, and be strong in your faith

(1 Peter 5:8,9 NLT)

Perhaps we need to look much more intently as to God's truthful view of sin. I believe the more we purpose to see sin as God sees it, the more conviction we will receive from the Holy Spirit and desire to flee from it. When we have a true awareness of the damning aspects of sin—all of sin, all that it hinders, and all the damage it causes—we will then have a much more profound appreciation of God's grace.

Many believe that God's grace came into play at the time of Christ. They look to the Old Testament period and see it as thousands of years of God's judgment upon rebellious people ... judgment and consequences. But the truth is that being gracious is part of God's character, which He has never been without. Grace was at no time added to God's list of defining attributes. Further, God being all-powerful and self-existing has never been in need of anything, nor can anything be added to Him or taken away. So, the grace of God has always been the same. Never any more or any less ... to think anything different would be to strip away the factuality of God's grace having been without beginning, and being never-ending and perfect in totality, immensity, and infinitude.

When God spoke the heavens, stars, planets, and earth into existence, His grace was displayed. When God created Adam in His image, grace was manifest into the life of mankind. When God created Eve from the side of Adam, God's grace provided a helpmate, companion, and lover to him. Before you were ever conceived, God created your soul to receive His Word of truth, His revelation of Himself. His grace was perfectly present and most freely given.

When we truly begin to see sin the way God sees it, when we truly understand the ramifications of sin, the spiritual death and damning eternal effects of sin ... then we are in the right position to truly understand and experience God's grace, His amazing grace ... and that should drive us to our knees, to bow our hearts before God in awe of His love, mercy, splendor, and glorious grace!

> If My people who are called by My name will humble themselves, and pray and seek My face, and turn from their wicked ways, then I will hear from heaven, and will forgive their sin and heal their land.
>
> (2 Chronicles 7:14 NKJV)

Without exception, one of the most powerful prayers I can pray is for God to reveal to me His truth regarding the areas of sin within my life that I need to repent of and turn to Him. I can tell you without hesitation, God has always been faithful to show me the specific sins that need immediate attention. Whatever might be grieving the Holy Spirit, the sins in my life that may hinder God using me for His intended purpose—the desires, discontents, or disobedient behaviors—God is *always* faithful to reveal and most eager to remove and restore, the moment I repent and rest in His forgiveness, grace, and love!

In Paul's letter to believers at Ephesus, he wrote a most beautiful prayer and I can think of no greater words more appropriately fitting to close this chapter than with those inspired by the Holy Spirit nearly two thousand years ago.

> For this reason I bow my knees to the Father of our Lord Jesus Christ, from whom the whole family in heaven and earth is named, that He would grant you, according to the riches of His glory, to be strengthened with might through His Spirit in the

inner man, that Christ may dwell in your hearts through faith; that you, being rooted and grounded in love, may be able to comprehend with all the saints what is the width and length and depth and height - to know the love of Christ which passes knowledge; that you may be filled with all the fullness of God.

(Ephesians 3:14–19 NKJV)

How great our need, that we might choose to abide in Christ in the forever-present moments, in *holy respiration* of life, filled with hearts overflowing of praise and worship unto Him in Spirit and in all truth.

Chapter 25

THE FAR SIDE OF LYRICS

Let's investigate yet another very important principle of our worship of God. What I'm about to convey to you comes from both personal observations and having experienced countless interactions with people in areas of worship and biblical instruction. Although I might have incorporated the following into chapter 12 under "secondhand worship," I felt compelled to convey this as a *standalone* biblical truth. What I'm about to impart to you is done so in hopes that you'll earnestly give deliberate thought to the relevant applications and ultimately become motivated by taking action.

First of all, I begin with this simple yet truthful fact for your consideration: *memorization is not the equivalent of one possessing knowledge or wisdom!*

Now, I believe there might be some people who would like to take that statement up for debate. Therefore, I fully intend to justify its factuality and relevance. I must admit, I never gave much consideration to that statement in my early years of musical endeavors, and it wasn't until recently that I discovered this to be a tremendous biblical truth.

To help establish the veracity of this principle, I ask you to pause for a few moments and consider the following notable songs. I would imagine you'll recognize at least one if not all of these incredibly popular hits: "Feliz Navidad" performed by Jose Feliciano, "Oye Como Va" by Carlos Santana, and "La Bamba," which was recorded by Ritchie Valens and later Los Lobos for the movie *La Bamba* soundtrack. All of these songs have received numerous awards and have topped the charts over the years. In my younger days of professional drumming, I performed these as cover tunes hundreds of times, perhaps more. I could sing every lyric of those songs, word for word … and yet, I didn't have a clue of what I was singing!

In point of fact, it's quite possible for a person to memorize a foreign language, repeating the various words and phrases and yet having absolutely no idea what they're communicating. For that matter, there are birds that can mimic speaking by repeating words without having any reasoning as to what they're saying.

That being said, I find it incredibly interesting to observe the number of people who are virtually enamored by certain persons who possess brilliant intellectual capacities and academic achievement. There appears to be an almost reverent awe held by many toward those who have a far greater IQ than that of the average person. Self-made billionaires often seem to perpetuate a certain mystique, which frequently promotes a type of idolization from those who follow their success. Those persons have been dubbed as having a *superiority of smarts* so to speak. However, I believe there is yet another biblical principle of truth that demands our earnest attention and that is that even the most educated persons of highly accredited institutions, those who have attained academic accolades and distinctions of title, may possess very little wisdom.

This was the obstacle of the Pharisees and Sadducees, as those boys couldn't see the forest for the trees. Even with all of their education, religious teachings, scholarly conversations, titles of position, authority, and wealth, most of them didn't have an ounce of wisdom within them when it came time to discern Christ's teachings. We do well to recognize that just because a person can assimilate huge amounts of information and recall those facts with pinpoint accuracy doesn't mean they have the ability to discern even the most simple, basic truths of God's Word and revelation of Himself. Let me state it again: *memorization is not the equivalent of one possessing knowledge or wisdom!*

It was sometime in the year 2007 that God opened up my eyes to show me the factuality of that statement and also began to reveal to me just how often I missed out on the deeper truths of both the lyrics of worship and truth of His Word. The fact that I could repeat a song lyric or Bible verse didn't mean I necessarily had a full understanding of the truth contained within its context—not to mention having enough wisdom to know how to make it applicable in my daily life.

It's amazing how frequently the songs we sing in church are repeated with very little attention given to the story behind the song ... the truth from which the lyrics were inspired being much more relevant than what we might assume. Not that every song has a hidden meaning or far greater message than we initially understand, but many of them do! We also discover this principle of truth within the study of God's Word. The deeper we examine the text and seek God's true meaning, the more we discover!

With that, I want to tell you about yet another personal experience to further convey the reality of how important and applicable all of this is to our worship.

One of my favorite hymns over the years has been, "It Is Well." It's grown on me over time and today is one that can be numbered among my top-ten favorite hymns. Even though I'm as deaf as a brick and can't hear a word or note I'm singing, I can recall this wonderful song from memory and sing it forth ... but not that I'd risk a public tone-deaf performance, mind you.

Now I need to pump the brakes here a second and be very transparent with you. I never liked hymns at all when I was younger. In fact, I was bored stupid when the choir would sing them, and I could hardly wait for them to be finished so the pastor could move on to the message for the day. Back in my younger days, I wanted some "happening'" music during the church service ... loud and fast, something with real rhythm! None of that mundane choral stuff. I wanted something a drummer could slam out some grooves and thump ... make me wanna jump up to my feet. Yeah, that's where I was in life, in all my naive youthful and uneducated understanding regarding worship.

But let me tell you something. As I grew older, the fondness of the lyrics and melodies of many of those old hymns, those treasured classics of the older folks, began to settle into my soul ... well beyond the limits of tempo, grooves, physical hearing, and repeating of the words, and into a far greater depth of apprehension.

Now, back to this hymn, "It Is Well." What a treasury it holds for the one who truly understands the depths of the heart from which it was written. To know the story behind this great song should leave a person in astonishment of how such enormous praise could be written from such a point in time of expectant overwhelming grief, loss, and sorrow of soul. The lyrics were written by Horatio G.

Spafford, a once most prominent Chicago lawyer. His testimony is one that every Christian should invest the time in which to become acquainted.

Additionally, if we look to a contemporary song for similar comparison, we can examine that of Matt Redman's, "The Heart of Worship." If you've been attending any of the evangelical contemporary worship services over the past ten years, it's pretty much a sure thing you've sung this song more than a few times. In fact, more than likely, you've sung many of his songs over the course of recent years and would be unaware that he was the composer. Matt is an amazing songwriter in my opinion, and he's truly gifted as a musician and profoundly anointed in his ministry of music. This song of his is yet another one that I love to sing from memory. Unlike the hymn "It Is Well," I embraced this song the first time I heard it—and yes, I just wrote the words, "heard it"!

You see, "The Heart of Worship," was at its pinnacle in popularity during the time I still had my hearing. The song didn't need to grow on me, not even a little! The melody and lyrics just grabbed hold of my heart from the onset! However, as I soon discovered, the story behind this song is what took me to a whole different level in my times of worship. The meaning of the lyrics began to unveil much more than words accompanying a melody. They in fact, were a message of truth being revealed to the heart of a believer, a worshipper, and I was one who needed the insights that God revealed to Matt.

Now, I chose purposefully during the writing of this chapter not to go into greater detail on the background of either of these two songs. I want to allow you the opportunity to discover on your own the true meanings and stories behind the lyrics you sing. I would encourage you to invest the time by searching the Internet. You can simply use your favorite search engine and type in the song title and composer and you'll be able to track down numerous links leading you into the testimonies of the respective author's composition.

To summarize for application here: I've discovered that when I invest the time to understand the lyrics, there is most often a genuine biblical truth to be learned. When I desire to greater understand the history and story behind the hymns and contemporary songs, those discoveries can bring about far greater impact than transposing the mere words about God on paper, and they can contribute to the authentic, heartfelt worship of God.

I pray that the forgoing thoughts will be of encouragement and inspiration to you! You can move beyond simply reading what was written and into purposed application.

It Is Well

When peace, like a river, attendeth my way,
When sorrows like sea billows roll;
Whatever my lot, Thou has taught me to say,
It is well, it is well, with my soul.

Though Satan should buffet, though trials should come,
Let this blest assurance control,
That Christ has regarded my helpless estate,
And hath shed His own blood for my soul.

My sin. Oh, the bliss of this glorious thought!
My sin, not in part but in whole,
Is nailed to the cross, and I bear it no more,
Praise the Lord, praise the Lord, O my soul!

And Lord haste the day when my faith shall be sight,
The clouds be rolled back as a scroll;
The trump shall resound, and the Lord shall descend,
Even so, it is well with my soul.
It is well, with my soul,
It is well, with my soul,
It is well, it is well, with my soul.[27]

---

[27] Horatio G. Spafford, "It Is Well with My Soul" (1873).

Chapter 26

BEYOND OUR CULTURE OF CHAOS

It's amazing what retrospective contemplation can accomplish in the life of a person willing to look truthfully in the mirror. When we seek in humility for God to reveal His truth to us, ever so frequently the fog in our thinking quickly disappears and we find ourselves looking upon a clear reflection. This certainly has been the case in my life on numerous occasions! Especially within the arena of my desire to follow God's will for my life, rather than getting all wrapped up in what I think I should be doing for Him.

I've found that through my times in prayerfully seeking to have balance in my life, God has always been faithful to show me the areas where I've veered off track and perhaps gone astray. It's through those times in desiring God's guidance that I've come to learn much of that which needs both attention and specific correction. From my personal testimony in dealing with the single barrier of busyness, nothing could have been more evident of God's faithful guidance than through the lessons I needed to learn.

The whole barrier of busyness amassed from all the chaos in my life was yet another most hindering obstacle for me. Not just in my times of worshipping God with others mind you, but in fact it was a most tragic monument within my overall lifestyle. The seriousness of this staggering blockade only became exposed as God began to strip away the various activities and accumulations of material possessions that had preoccupied the majority of my time.

One by one, as they were being removed, I began to realize the overwhelming toll this barrier had taken upon me. My being driven by productivity, achieving something, having something, doing something … busy, busy, busy. I was either actively involved doing something, or doing something to become actively involved later. Let me tell you, if someone were looking for a poster person to epitomize living within the culture of chaos and being bombarded by busyness, I would've been a strong candidate.

However, as I mentioned earlier, God graciously removed those damming blockages one by one from my life. And through that process, not only have I become much more sensitive to observing the effects of busyness on a personal level, but also looking intently at the utter chaos of such busyness, which impedes so much of our society. Through my increased interest and concern in this area, I began to have greater in-depth conversations with people, focusing on the challenges they face in prioritizing their schedules and frequently learning how the demanding pressures of life have taken away time with God, being with family and friends. A most alarming and significant toll upon countless families has been rendered from such busyness. The more I conversed and purposed to study, the more I began to discover the magnitude of how epidemic it's become within our culture.

Our society operates to a cadence of hectic schedules, trying to fulfill all of the demanding obligations required of us. People are run ragged from one activity to the next. There are seemingly unending things to accomplish on our to-do lists and as one gets checked off, another two are added. It's no wonder why we've become a society ravaged with anxiety and panic attacks. Multitudes of people are virtually collapsing from exhaustion in trying to meet the demands of the day. I assume you can more than identify with this and perhaps you've experienced such fatigue yourself a time or two as well.

One of the things I truly enjoy doing these days is to ask of people how I might specifically pray for them and be of encouragement in their lives. By far, the number one prayer request is centered on the issue of "finding balance in life." I've discovered there's a common thread among people desiring to find rest, peace, and relief from all the pressures and demands that are upon them.

Not only is this true in the day-to-day schedules of countless people, this also holds significant relevance for the schedules of those in ministry. To take the already near overwhelming chaotic calendars of demands and add to them the involvement of ministry service can leave a great number of folks either burned out or not interested. It's been through such seasons in my life and through prayerfully seeking balance that the Holy Spirit has been ever so faithful to remind me that there is a most delicate balance between *doing* work for God and *being* with God. Did you catch that? If you're reading through right now at a fast pace, please slow down! I'm going to state that again here for you: *there's a most delicate balance between doing work for God and being with God!*

Often, I find that God will use the voice of others to show me a truth that so desperately needs application within my life. And it seems as the years roll by, the more reminders I need. Such was the case in my reading *We Would See Jesus*. In their marvelous book, Roy and Revel Hession give strong encouragement to the reprioritizing of Christian service. Their message is great medicine for the soul of the individual believer, and it also would well serve the church as a whole today:

> We direly need to leave our lusting for ever larger spheres of Christian service and concentrate on seeing God for ourselves and finding the deep answer for life in Him ... Our service of help to our fellows then becomes incidental to our vision of God and, ideally, the direct consequence of it. This does not mean that God does not want us engaged actively in His service. He does; but His purpose is often far different from what we think. Our service, in His mind, is to be far more the potter's wheel on which He can mold us than the achieving of those spectacular objectives on which we set our hearts.[28]

Wow! How I wished I would have come into possession of this book in my early years of ministry service. It's not a new book by any means as the original text was first published in 1958. Yet I firmly believe the truth of its message is most critical to be received by the church today! More so than any other time throughout church history, we've become activity driven. The promulgating of programs transpiring within most North American churches is mind-boggling. And I believe what is essential for the individual believer is equally imperative for the collective body.

---

28   Roy and Revel Hession, *We Would See Jesus* (CLC Publications: Fort Washington, PA), 23. Used by permission.

Chapter 27

HEADING TO THE HARVEST—SOW WHAT?

Our society has become so focused on the ideologies of having a solid return on investment (ROI) that little else seems to gauge our measurement of success. Certainly and without equivocation this applies to the business world and all secular financial investing. From purchasing stock on the exchange market, to contributing to 401(k)s, to having company shares as part of annual compensation, or for those people banking on a sole proprietorship, all of us have the common collective question of, What's my return on investment going to be? Let's face the truth and acknowledge that the vast majority of us want to see tangible results from where we invest our time, money, and energies.

One of the most prevalent lessons I've discovered regarding this mind-set stems from a biblical truth of understanding that is contrasting in nature; that being, the principal difference between *sowing* and *reaping*. Our current culture, both secular society and that of many churches, is to be "reaping" minded, or looking toward the return of investment of our activities and our labors. There is absolute biblical foundation here for having a "reaps" mindedness as we look to the gospel of John within the fourth chapter. We find Jesus telling His disciples that He receives heavenly food and nourishment as He purposes to fulfill the work of the Father.

> Jesus said to them, "My food is to do the will of him who sent me and to accomplish his work. Do you not say, 'There are yet four months, then comes the harvest'? Look, I tell you, lift up your eyes, and see that the fields are white for harvest. Already the one who reaps is receiving wages and gathering fruit for eternal life, so that sower and reaper may rejoice together. For the saying holds true, 'One sows and another reaps.'"

(John 4:34–37 ESV)

Now stay with me on this, as we need to examine a significant contrasting principle, which I'm afraid many people today within the church have overlooked. The key here is found in the second part of verse 37: "One sows and another reaps." That's truth, from Christ Jesus to us. That single word, *another*, is of huge significance for us to apprehend. Some of us will be sowing, while others will be reaping. And yes, sometimes we will both sow and reap. However, why is it that we've become so preoccupied with the "reaping" aspect of ministry over and above the "sowing"?

As I was finishing the final chapters of this book, I met with my dear friend Torrey Larsen. It was during our lunch conversation while we were discussing my book, when he asked me this specific question: "Tim, why is it that we've become so focused on reaping rather than sowing, why is that?" I began to tell him from my personal observation and discovery that "I believe it's from the secular ROI mind-set being used to determine success, which now has infiltrated into our ministry activities for God." We, the church, want to see more people in the seats each week, more first-time commitments, more people in Sunday school classes, more folks in small groups, bigger and better programs for our families. We want to see the results ... and the sooner the better! The fact is, most churches have become ROI preoccupied.

But let's stop here and I want to present something for you to think about. During that same lunch meeting with Torrey, he hit me up with a statement that I feel we should all have engraved on a plaque to read every day. He wrote these words down on paper for me, to make sure I didn't miss what he was trying to tell me: "Think about the preacher who led Billy Graham to Christ." Wow! The first thoughts that came to my mind were, *That's a sower right there! Faithful to serve! Focused on obedience rather than just results!* That minister of God's Word sowed a seed in young Billy's life as a teenager, which has brought forth countless fruit, unfathomable impact, and multitudes only God can number. And yet, I would venture to say, that as that evangelist minister was about to preach during the tent revival meeting that evening, he wasn't approaching the pulpit with a question of, "What's in this for me tonight?"

I discovered a most interesting article from the archives of *Harper's Magazine* dating back to 1975. From the research he conducted, Dr. Herbert Hendin detailed his discoveries of the social barriers between young men and women on campuses. What he discusses in his article still provides great relevance for us today:

> It is no accident that at the present time the dominant trends in psycho-analysis are the rediscovery of narcissism and the new emphasis on the psychological significance of death. The

society is marked by a self-interest and egocentrism that increasingly reduces all relations to the question, "What am I getting out of it?" Nothing blocks involvement more effectively than the sense that anything felt or done for another person is a wearisome burden or that nothing is worthwhile that does not immediately result in some gain. The general fascination with self-aggrandizement persuades many more young people to judge relationships by the points they can win or lose.[29]

Nearly four decades later, it most certainly seems the previous social concerns of that generation has now permeated in most areas of our society today. How many of us have asked these questions either verbally or internally: What's my return going to be from all this and when can I expect to see it? What's in it for me? What do I get out of all this?

Strikingly different are the activities and experiences between the one who sows and the one who reaps. Consider the following contrasts:

Persons who are primarily focused on "reaping" typically desire to enjoy the gratification of accomplishment, seeing the immediate results within their lifetime. Some enjoy the accolades and recognition of their labors. Others are motivated by witnessing the physical numerical and spiritual growth, while others may be purposed toward the financial increases and availing opportunities arising from those gains.

When considering the "sowers," those people whose main objectives are to diligently and prayerfully seek God's will, being obedient and faithful, who live by faith and are willing to sacrifice self for serving God regardless of the cost, theirs is a determined

---

29 *Harper's Magazine* (August 1975). Issue by special permission.

life to work the soil and plant the seeds. Their "reaping" most often comes from the blessing in knowing that they're following God's will and purpose for their lives during that exact time and season.

The balancing between the two, that of sowing and reaping, should be on the forefront of all our ministry undertakings … all of our busyness in life. We need to pause often and consider the eternal implications and return on our investments beyond that of just the temporal. We would do well to purpose our thoughts toward the vertical in view of a divine perspective rather than just that of a horizontal dividend.

Living out our faith in holy worship on a continual basis requires ongoing evaluation. It involves a willingness to step back from a focal point of our human doings for God and examine our times of being with God. We can never afford to lose the truth, that God is seeking us—those who will worship Him in spirit and truth! God is seeking us! He is seeking me! He is seeking you!

Knowing that no harvest can come without the working of the ground and sowing of the seed, my prayer would be for us as a body of believers to become ever so mindful of the need for both and to willingly do either the sowing or reaping as cheerful, obedient, and humble servants. For it is within such service, that a most profound act of worship is to be discovered. One which will bless others and glorify God!

> Let us turn and examine our ways, and return to the Lord! Let us lift up our hearts and hands to God in heaven.
>
> (Lamentations 3:40–41 ESV)

Chapter 28

From Repression To Revival

The world is perishing for lack of the knowledge of God and the Church is famishing for want of His Presence. The instant cure of most of our religious ills would be to enter the Presence in spiritual experience, to become suddenly aware that we are in God and that God is in us.[30]

We desperately need to understand the vast differences in our being able to approach the throne of God *with confidence* and not *in our casualness* toward His character. In Christ, we've been given the ability to approach God *with boldness*, yet never *in our brazenness*. We must never allow ourselves to confuse having the gift of *holy familiarity* and thereby try to exchange it with an *irreverent flippancy*. It's a most tragic and unfortunate unholy flippancy that today plagues our nation and a great number of the houses of worship.

---

30   A. W. Tozer, *The Pursuit of God* (1948).

The sweetness of God's presence, peace, and solace that once filled so many sanctuaries has now resulted in the frequent absence of the Holy Spirit's workings and God's manifest presence among the people. Perhaps now more than ever, we should earnestly look to God's Word, follow His instruction, and eagerly await His promise!

For many, the word *revival* seems to spark within them an almost mystical anticipation of God's working in a supernatural wave of radical transformation. They desire for a movement to transpire with unprecedented rivalry and unmatched experience, often looking for the restoration of the church within the areas where it has diminished in its work of saving souls. Revival means converting the masses of those unsaved and awakening with new fervency the hearts of the weary. Certainly, such miraculous occurrences have transpired several times over the history of the church, thereby creating within many of us the expectation that it will happen again.

However, today there seems to be a resistance to revival beginning within the life of one person. There appears to be a far greater interest for revival to transpire in many persons at once, rather than the one individual. We seemingly appear to be looking for the all-encompassing swoop of the Holy Spirit, rather than the individual encounter. In his book, *The Calvary Road*, Roy Hession provides his amazing insights into the meaning of revival:

> Now a word about Revival itself ... The common conception of Revival is usually that of a spectacular religious awakening, in which large numbers of the unconverted are convicted of sin and brought to Christ amid a good deal of excitement. Such a visitation of God's Spirit, while greatly to be desired, is thought to be largely unaccountable. It is something for which one can only pray and we must wait for it in God's good

time … Revival is just the life of the Lord Jesus poured into human hearts.[31]

I find those words to be so powerful and full of practical relevance for applying to my prayers in desire for revival to break forth. Rather than being preoccupied, consumed, and driven to experience the spectacular, I'd do far better in my walk with Christ to continually focus my prayers, to have the Lord Jesus poured into my heart. Consider this: if a local church assembly were to become solely purposed for such individual authentic experiences whereby the Lord Jesus was being poured into the heart of the individual believer, and one by one the outpouring of Christ was filling hearts, I believe that body of believers would truly be in the midst of the spectacular, the beginning of another great awakening and revival.

> Give unto the Lord the glory due to His name; Worship the Lord in the beauty of holiness.
>
> (Psalm 29:2 NKJV)
>
> Oh come, let us worship and bow down; Let us kneel before the Lord our Maker.
>
> (Psalm 95:6 NKJV)
>
> All the angels stood around the throne and the elders and the four living creatures, and fell on their faces before the throne and worshiped God, saying: "Amen! Blessing and glory and wisdom, Thanksgiving and honor and power and might, Be to our God forever and ever. Amen."
>
> (Revelation 7:11–12 NKJV)

---

31 Roy and Revel Hession, *The Calvary Road* (CLC Publishers: Fort Washington, PA). Kindle eBook; preface used by permission.

Chapter 29

BEFORE JOHN 3:16

Recently, I was working on a Bible study outline from the book of John. In doing so, I was suddenly taken in by two verses that I'd never previously studied with any significant focus. I'm not overly surprised in my not having examined those particular verses in great detail since the verse that follows is one of the most quoted verses from the entire Bible.

Most Christians today can recite John 3:16, as well they should. That verse is the very word of Christ speaking to a Jewish teacher by the name of Nicodemus who was truly interested in becoming born again (from above) and asking how a person could enter the kingdom of heaven. Nicodemus asked three questions, but when he specifically asked Christ, "How can these things be?" it is there at that point in their conversation that we find Jesus' answer, and it isn't just John 3:16. Christ's answer is found in John chapter 3, verses 10 through 21.

However, I want to focus on just three of the verses within Christ's answer, as I'm convicted these are the central remedy for our becoming authentic worshippers of God and the beginning of experiencing a new revival.

As I mentioned earlier, arguably one of the most recognized Scripture verses in the entire Bible comes from the book of John:

> For God so loved the world, that he gave his only Son, that whoever believes in him should not perish but have eternal life.

(3:16 ESV)

However, there are the two verses prior to John 3:16 that I desire to draw your attention:

> And as Moses lifted up the serpent in the wilderness, so must the Son of Man be lifted up, that whoever believes in him may have eternal life.

(3:14–15 ESV)

Now, for us to fully understand these verses, we need to examine the Old Testament passage and story from which Christ was speaking. It comes from Numbers 21:4–9.

Within this passage, we discover a most tragic event as the people of Israel had become impatient on their journey from Mount Hor. They became disgruntled and started grumbling and complaining against both God and Moses. So God sent fiery serpents among the people. They were bitten, became sick with a raging fever, and a great number of the people died. They were hemmed in, surrounded on all sides. There was no escaping the plague of serpents that God sent upon them as a result of their impatient attitude and for speaking against Him and His servant Moses.

But, in the midst of their rebellion and complacency, Moses went and prayed to God for the people, and God told Moses to make a bronze fiery serpent and set it on a pole, "and it shall be that everyone who is bitten, when he looks at it, shall live."[32] And what do you suppose happened next? "So Moses made a bronze serpent, and put it on a pole; and so it was, if a serpent had bitten anyone, when he looked at the bronze serpent, he lived."[33]

Now, perhaps you're asking yourself the following questions: How does this apply to the church today? How is this relevant to the barriers we've built up, in our having turned away from the rightful worship due God? Well, let's consider what we've just studied from the above story.

We too, like the people of Israel have become impatient. We don't wait for anything in this day and age. Fast food; rapid downloads of movies, books, and music; instant world access via the Internet; able to reach any phone anywhere in the world in just a few seconds ... we don't wait for anything! We've become a society of instant gratification. And to our own detriment, rarely do we wait on the Holy Spirit to do His work during our worship time.

We're just way too impatient in all areas of Christian life and have lost the understanding of what it means to wait upon the Lord. Couple this with the current criteria of normalcies for corporate worship, which emphasize entertainment, and then add to this our spirit of complacency and lethargy, and we too now find ourselves surrounded by serpents.

From all sides, we find ourselves being besieged by the Enemy, the painful bites from his attackers have resulted in many a church's spiritual death. We only need to consider the number of church doors closing each year, the divorce rates among professed

---

[32] Numbers 21:8 NKJV
[33] Numbers 21:9 NKJV

Christian couples, and the numbers of people who've abandoned their faith to realize the impact of these afflictions.

At the same time, we can't afford to give up nor continue with indifference. With the coming age of the New Testament church, Christ promised His followers that where two or three were gathered together in His name, He would be present (Matthew 18:20). No longer would the Jewish laws of sacrifice and tabernacle mandates be required of God to manifest His Shekinah glory.

When we think of church—or to make it personal, when I think of church—I need to get away from a multitude mind-set (lots of people) and focus on the two or three who are willing to come together and worship God acceptably. Just a few people coming together in seeking His presence can bring about a powerful change! That's of critical importance, because today I believe the remedy for removing the barriers within our churches, small groups, and home groups and within any assembly still remains the same as it did when Christ answered Nicodemus:

> And as Moses lifted up the serpent in the wilderness, so must the Son of Man be lifted up, that whoever believes in him may have eternal life.
>
> (John 3:14–15 NKJV)

We must look to Christ and consider the cross! We need to acknowledge and confess of our having often pursued avenues of self-pleasing entertainment during our times of worship gatherings. We have to examine what we allow to transpire within the house of God and prayerfully ask if that which we offer is biblically acceptable.

The cross of Christ, the blood He shed, His death, His burial, His resurrection and accession ... there's no entertainment in any of it. Christ's life was given in love and offered up by grace—but not for the purpose of popularity. It was with the purpose to penetrate the heart and soul. To pierce the prideful heart of sinful mankind! He came as our Savior, Redeemer, and High Priest in order to forgive our sins in atonement for what was to be our due judgment and to reconcile us back to God the Father.

On the knees of our heart is the best way to enter into His presence, in awful fear ... full of awe, astonishment, and wonder.

> Therefore, brethren, having boldness to enter the Holiest by the blood of Jesus, by a new and living way which He consecrated for us, through the veil, that is, His flesh, and having a High Priest over the house of God, let us draw near with a true heart in full assurance of faith, having our hearts sprinkled from an evil conscience and our bodies washed with pure water. Let us hold fast the confession of our hope without wavering, for He who promised is faithful. And let us consider one another in order to stir up love and good works, not forsaking the assembling of ourselves together, as is the manner of some, but exhorting one another, and so much the more as you see the Day approaching.
>
> (Hebrews 10:19–25 NKJV)

Chapter 30

FORWARD IN PRAYER: A PROGRESSION OF WORSHIP

Prayer is yet another incredibly powerful form of worship and should permeate the life of the believer and most certainly our times of assembly. Let's not forget that when Christ rebuked the money changers and sellers within the temple, He was quoting from the words of Isaiah, "My house shall be called a house of prayer"[34] (Matthew 21:13; Mark 11:17; Luke 19:46).

We need to remember that the church is far more than just a gathering of believers who serve, edify, and equip one another. Our coming together in the power of prayer unifies us in one accord. It's through our prayers in the name of Christ Jesus and the powerful workings of the Holy Spirit that Satan is overcome and his divisive schemes are thwarted. Each time we assemble, even just two or

---

34 Isaiah 56:7

three coming together, the prayers being bound on earth ascend to the throne of God.

Prayer is the means of our verbal faith in which we praise, petition, and proclaim our innermost thoughts, with confidence unto the Father. Praying enlarges our hearts, increases our faith, and causes us to often reflect upon others, both in supplication and in admiration to answered prayer. It teaches us how to persevere, how to become patient, and how to align our wills to that of God's for His glory. Through prayer, we learn selflessness as we make known our requests and the heartfelt burdens we carry for others, those that are above our own needs.

Prayer identifies our dependency on God and our admission that we're incapable and powerless without His direct intervention on our behalf. Genuine prayer, when offered from our total being, from our spirit and in truth, reflects our humility and reverence before God. Truly, this is one of the most powerfully personal forms of worship we can offer up to God the Father, in the name of Christ Jesus and through the power of the Holy Spirit.

When we seek God with authentic faith, with a confident eager expectation of unswerving hope and from the depths of a loving heart, God is pleased and rejoices in our having sought to be with Him. From the depths of a truthful prayer come the tender soul-baring words, the private expressions of the heart, too personal to ever be uttered in public. Yet these are the most sweet-sounding utterances to God in heaven.

> And when you pray, you must not be like the hypocrites. For they love to stand and pray in the synagogues and at the street corners, that they may be seen by others. Truly I say to you, they have received their reward. But when you pray, go into your room and shut the door and pray to your

> Father who is in secret. And your Father who sees in secret will reward you.
>
> (Matthew 6:5–7 ESV)

> Is anyone among you suffering? Let him pray. Is anyone cheerful? Let him sing psalms. Is anyone among you sick? Let him call for the elders of the church, and let them pray over him, anointing him with oil in the name of the Lord. And the prayer of faith will save the sick, and the Lord will raise him up. And if he has committed sins, he will be forgiven. Confess your trespasses to one another, and pray for one another, that you may be healed. The effective, fervent prayer of a righteous man avails much.
>
> (James 5:13–16 NKJV)

We must never lose sight that God can be equally worshipped in the mightiest shouts of praise and in the silence and stillness of the heart. God examines the internal position of the heart long before the proclamation is ever heard. Genuine spiritual worship comes from within, where the heart, mind, and soul have been joined with God. It's the internal attitude (not the external activities) that pleases God most during our time of intimate fellowship with Him.

God so graciously and lovingly welcomes us to come into His presence! Christ tells us to abide in Him (John 15:4), to abide in His words (verse 7), and to abide in His love (verse 9). He knows us by name (10:3, 14) and calls us friend (15:15), therefore we have the great assurance we can approach His throne with a holy familiarity, where we can never wear out our welcome nor overstay being in His holy presence! How great the need for believer's today, to realize that for us to seek to abide in anything but Christ Jesus will never be enough!

Prayer Is the Soul's Sincere Desire

Prayer is the soul's sincere desire, unuttered or expressed;
The motion of a hidden fire, that trembles in the breast.
Prayer is the burden of a sigh, the falling of a tear
The upward glancing of an eye, when none but God is near.

Prayer is the Christian's vital breath, the Christian's native air,
His watchword at the gates of death; he enters heaven with prayer.
O Thou, by Whom we come to God, the Life, the Truth, the Way;
The path of prayer Thyself hast trod: Lord, teach us how to pray!

Prayer is the contrite sinner's voice, returning from his ways,
While angels in their songs rejoice, and cry, "Behold, he prays!"
The saints in prayer appear as one, in word, in deed, and mind,
While with the Father and the Son, sweet fellowship they find.

No prayer is made by man alone, the Holy Spirit pleads,
And Jesus, on th'eternal throne, for sinners intercedes.
O Thou by Whom we come to God, the Life, the Truth, the Way,
The path of prayer Thyself hast trod: Lord, teach us how to pray.[35]

---

35 "Prayer Is the Soul's Sincere Desire," lyrics by James Montgomery (1816).

Chapter 31

THE JOURNEY OF OBEDIENCE: EVIDENCE OF WORSHIP

> Today, if you hear his voice, do not harden your hearts.
>
> (Hebrews 4:7 ESV)

> Although he was a son, he learned obedience through what he suffered. And being made perfect, he became the source of eternal salvation to all who obey him...
>
> (Hebrews 5:8–9 ESV)

Obedience unto the Lord is also a tremendous form of worship! Our willingness to obey God's Word, follow His leading, and submit to His will is our actionable testimony. Nothing gives greater evidence to the life of a true believer in Christ Jesus than that of their obedience unto the Lord.

Ralph Waldo Emerson proclaimed this great statement: "Who you are speaks so loudly I can't hear what you're saying." That's the dynamic persona of a believer who is so full of the Holy Spirit that his cup is splashing out all over the place and where their verbal testimony is secondary to their actions.

Obedience—it's not a real popular word in our culture. Neither is the word *submissive*. Most people want to talk about their independence and liberties in life. They want to exercise their free will and rights under the laws of our country's Constitution and grace under God. Our culture screams of self-sufficiency and becoming your own person. Be all that you can be and more than you can imagine ... never be content with the person you are or where you are in life. Those ideologies have elevated our self-sins far beyond the joyful acceptance of being obedient, submissive, and eagerly serving God as He wills for our life.

The contrary aspect of obedience to God is our self-will taking priority and in that mind-set, no revival can ever transpire. Looking out for number one, when number one is myself, will bring nothing but distance in my relationship with God, family, and friends. Being "lonely at the top" holds a great truth for those who follow their own agenda and pursue it to make their own destiny.

> Discord and discontent among believers is rooted within the soil of disobedience to God.

It would be well to our advantage to mull over the observations of Charles Finney (1792–1875).

> When there are dissensions, and jealousies, and evil speakings among professors of religion, then there is great need of revival. These things show

that Christians have got far from God, and it is time to think earnestly of a revival ... A revival is nothing else than a new beginning of obedience to God.

Powerful is Finney's definition of revival ... and it begs us to give careful consideration! Nothing mystical or a supernatural fire from heaven type thing ... nope! Pure, simple, and straightforward: *a revival is nothing more than a new beginning of obedience to God.* Scores of folks might well be seeking revival most earnestly, yet more than likely, far fewer of them are willing to be totally obedient to God.

> The Lord of Heaven's Armies says to the priests: "A son honors his father, and a servant respects his master. If I am your father and master, where are the honor and respect I deserve?"
>
> (Malachi 1:6 NLT)
>
> With a servant, a warrior, a child, or a subject, obedience is indispensable, the first sign of integrity. And shall God, the living, glorious God, find no obedience with us? No, let cheerful, timely, precise, obedience from the beginning be the evidence of the genuineness of our fellowship with the Son whose obedience is our life.[36]

Obedience, the new beginning of revival, will not happen by chance or through osmosis. Obedience requires a predisposition and resolve of personal commitment. And our commitment to God must preside over our momentary feelings about God! Following

---

36 From *The Essential Works of Andrew Murray*, published by Barbour Publishing, Inc. Used by permission." Page 251.

God's will and instructions shouldn't occur only when we feel like it or when we're feeling the emotions of love and desire to be obedient. Rather, it should stem from a conscience discipline based upon unwavering steadfast devotion.

Chapter 32

Crossing from Commitment to Feelings

This was yet another tremendous insight God showed me regarding my worship, which is magnified through my actions of obedience unto Him. And the critical truth of this has had a most profound impact upon my overall relationship with God, my wife, my children, and those whom I most treasure as friends.

Sorrowfully, I must admit there was a time where I wasn't feeling any of the emotions of love in any aspect of my life—no excitement, no joy, no enthusiasm, no love, nothing … nada, zip. That's a dangerous spot to be in for sure, and I can admit in truth to you, in the void of emotions came the filler of indifference. And when indifference, apathy, or lethargy runs full, there's little room for obedience.

When a Christian tries to live among the shadows of the world, sooner or later a choice will have to be made. Either they'll run to the light of Christ in repentance or try to find cover in the darkness of rebellion. And let me tell you, playing in the shadows is no place for a Christian to seek fulfillment in life. There's no margin for latitude, for a genuine, passionate Christ follower to be contently living in semi-obedience to God!

What I discovered through that season was that my obedience to God requires both apprehension of His Word and application of it. Being emotionally motivated or having feelings of love is not the criteria for being obedient to God. My commitment to God is the source from which I need to muster up and follow His instruction. God already knows my deepest sentiments and regardless of those feelings, my commitment should remain unshakeable. I've discovered when I'm not in possession of the emotions or motivations, if I do the actions with the right mind-set, the feelings typically will follow. Simply put: actions first, feelings follow! In some cases it might take longer than at other times for the feelings or motivation to catch up, but the application has yet to fail me.

Look it at like this: if you begin a diet and eat the prescribed foods to lose weight and you remain faithful, you'll lose weight. If you start a weight-lifting regimen and stick to it, you'll get stronger. If you commence taking piano lessons and practice, you'll learn to play the piano. Actions first, results follow … Actions first, feelings follow! This is a huge imperative for us to realize when it comes to our relationships! To examine this concept from a progressive linear approach, it simply looks like this:

Commitment ➔ Actions ➔ Feelings ➔ Results

Our commitment is what should compel us to remain faithful to God. This in turn should create within us a desire to be obedient in our actions. As we seek in all areas to follow Christ in humility and in spirit and truth, the love of God will flow through us. Our worshipful living will bless God, and the Holy Spirit will bring forth heavenly blessing within our lives.

Perhaps some of what's been lost among so many Christians today is the understanding of these very principles. They're waiting on the feeling to drive the actions and then get the results. And if the feelings and results are okay with them, then they'll stay committed. Further, for many, they're resting their beliefs upon seeing results first and then they'll increase their faith accordingly. But that's never going to work, and if left unchecked or unchanged, it will only bring about discouragement and discontent in their faith.

Prayer and obedience: our investment into the lives of other believers; equipping the saints; edifying and loving one another; giving of our time, talents, and treasures; abstaining from various desires; seeking and submitting to the will of God are all actions of worship. They're not suggestions for the disciple of Christ; they're loving, life-filled spiritual requirements! These are the evidences of our faith and are themselves tangible forms of worship unto God. Further, we aren't afforded the leeway of being able to pick and choose, which actions we want to obey. They're not to be separated and if we believe such practices would adhere to a life marked out by obedience, then we only fool ourselves.

I really like the way George Müller provided some discourse about this particular concern:

> Faith has nothing to do with feelings or with impressions, with improbabilities or with outward experiences. If we desire to couple such things with faith, then we are no longer resting on the Word of God, because faith needs nothing of the kind. Faith

rests on the naked Word of God. When we take Him at His Word, the heart is at peace.[37]

When we come to this continual worship-filled living through our committed obedience, it becomes what Charles Spurgeon referred to as "holy respiration." Just as we inhale and exhale, so too we can both give prayer and praise, seeking God's will and then our being obedient to it, one followed by the other. A heart that is truly filled with praise will soon be revealed from the lips. I can't think of a greater example of this than where it is recorded in Luke's gospel about Mary being told by the angel Gabriel that she was chosen to be the mother of the Messiah, the Savior of the world, the Son of God. After submitting to the Lord's will for her life, she speaks forth in tremendous praise.[38]

> Mary responded, "Oh, how my soul praises the Lord. How my spirit rejoices in God my Savior! For he took notice of his lowly servant girl, and from now on all generations will call me blessed. For the Mighty One is holy, and he has done great things for me. He shows mercy from generation to generation to all who fear him. His mighty arm has done tremendous things! He has scattered the proud and haughty ones. He has brought down princes from their thrones and exalted the humble. He has filled the hungry with good things and sent the rich away with empty hands. He has helped his servant Israel and remembered to be merciful. For he made this promise to our ancestors, to Abraham and his children forever."
>
> (Luke 1:46–55 NLT)

---

[37] George Müller (1805–1898).
[38] Luke 1:26–35

Section 4

Inspiration Toward Holy Worship

Chapter 33

SEVEN INDISPENSIBLE TRUTHS OF ACCEPTABLE WORSHIP

Along my life's journey of prayerful study in seeking to worship God in a manner holy and acceptable to Him, I've learned there are some very relevant actions that we can do in preparation for offering authentic worship to God. In addition to our times of prayer, obedience, and self-sacrifice, which are of utmost importance, we must incorporate what I believe to be seven biblical imperatives. No doubt, the person who practices these biblical principles on a regular basis will move toward a greater intimacy with God. When groups of believers become devoted to such practice, I believe they will experience newfound spiritual revival in their congregations and become transformed by the manifest presence of God during their times of corporate worship.

1. **Our hearts must be filled with love and sincere adoration for God.**

    Jesus said to him, "You shall love the Lord your God with all your heart, with all your soul, and with all your mind."

    (Matthew 22:37 NKJV)

2. **We must seek God's presence with eager anticipation.**

    For we through the Spirit eagerly wait for the hope of righteousness by faith.

    (Galatians 5:5 NKJV)

3. **We must not be preoccupied with the external.**

    Therefore, my beloved, flee from idolatry.

    (1 Corinthians 10:14 NKJV)

    For you shall worship no other god, for the Lord, whose name is Jealous, is a jealous God.

    (Exodus 34:14 NKJV)

4. **We must be willing to yield to the Holy Spirit.**

    Let no corrupting talk come out of your mouths, but only such as is good for building up, as fits the occasion, that it may give grace to those who hear. And do not grieve the Holy Spirit of God, by whom you were sealed for the day of redemption. Let all bitterness and wrath and anger and clamor and slander be put away from you, along with all malice.

    (Ephesians 4:29–31 ESV)

> Rejoice always, pray without ceasing, give thanks in all circumstances; for this is the will of God in Christ Jesus for you. Do not quench the Spirit.
>
> (1 Thessalonians 5:16–19 NKJV)
>
> For those who live according to the flesh set their minds on the things of the flesh, but those who live according to the Spirit, set their minds on the things of the Spirit.
>
> (Romans 8:5 ESV)

5. **We must confess if we harbor anything within us that displeases God.**

   > Therefore if you bring your gift to the altar, and there remember that your brother has something against you, leave your gift there before the altar, and go your way. First be reconciled to your brother, and then come and offer your gift.
   >
   > (Matthew 5:23–24 NKJV)

6. **We must realize that the total sum of all creatures in heaven exists to worship God.**

   > All the angels stood around the throne and the elders and the four living creatures, and fell on their faces before the throne and worshiped God, saying: "Amen! Blessing and glory and wisdom, Thanksgiving and honor and power and might, Be to our God forever and ever. Amen."
   >
   > (Revelation 7:11–12 NKJV)

7. **We must come with hearts of reverence, filled with wonder, awe, and astonishment.**

> Therefore, since we are receiving a kingdom which cannot be shaken, let us have grace, by which we may serve God acceptably with reverence and godly fear.
>
> (Hebrews 12:28 NKJV)

Chapter 34

SEVEN REVERENT POSTURES OF A WORSHIPFUL HEART

In addition to the seven biblical actions outlined in the previous chapter, we must contemplate our mental mind-sets, our positional thinking in order to engage in an internal reverent posture as we come before the throne of almighty God.

1. **Our internal posture, kneeling before God in spirit—contrite and reverent**

   > Behold, You desire truth in the inward parts, And in the hidden part You will make me to know wisdom … Create in me a clean heart O God, and renew a steadfast spirit within me … For You do not desire sacrifice, or else I would give it; You do not delight in burnt offering. The sacrifices of God

are a broken spirit, A broken and contrite heart—
These, O God, You will not despise.

(Psalm 51:6, 10, 16–17 NKJV)

2. **Our position of internal thoughts and inward reflections and affections**

   Now to Him who is able to do exceedingly abundantly above all that we ask or think, according to the power that works in us, to Him be glory in the church by Christ Jesus to all generations, forever and ever. Amen.

   (Ephesians 3:20–21 NKJV)

   For the weapons of our warfare are not carnal but mighty in God for pulling down strongholds, casting down arguments and every high thing that exalts itself against the knowledge of God, bringing every thought into captivity to the obedience of Christ.

   (2 Corinthians 10:4–5 NKJV)

3. **Having genuine humility—this is not thinking less of ourselves, rather just thinking of ourselves a lot less often**

   For I say, through the grace given to me, to everyone who is among you, not to think of himself more highly than he ought to think, but to think soberly, as God has dealt to each one a measure of faith.

   (Romans 12:3 NKJV)

> Therefore, as the elect of God, holy and beloved, put on tender mercies, kindness, humility, meekness, longsuffering.
>
> (Colossians 3:12 NKJV)
>
> I, therefore, the prisoner of the Lord, beseech you to walk worthy of the calling with which you were called, with all lowliness and gentleness, with longsuffering, bearing with one another in love, endeavoring to keep the unity of the Spirit in the bond of peace.
>
> (Ephesians 4:1–3 NKJV)

4. **Worshipping in truth—being honest with God in all areas of our lives**

   > I appeal to you therefore, brothers, by the mercies of God, to present your bodies as a living sacrifice, holy and acceptable to God, which is your spiritual worship. Do not be conformed to this world, but be transformed by the renewal of your mind, that by testing you may discern what is the will of God, what is good and acceptable and perfect.
   >
   > (Romans 12:1–2 ESV)
   >
   > O Lord, you have searched me and you know me. You know when I sit and when I rise; you perceive my thoughts from afar. You discern my going out and my lying down; you are familiar with all my ways. Before a word is on my tongue you know it completely, O Lord… Where can I go from your Spirit? Where can I flee from your presence?
   >
   > (Psalm 139:1–3, 7 NIV)

5. **Being filled with a transcendent wonder and holy fear of the Lord God**

> Tremble, O earth, at the presence of the Lord, At the presence of the God of Jacob.
>
> (Psalm 114:7 NKJV)
>
> Who is like you, O Lord, among the gods? Who is like you, majestic in holiness, awesome in glorious deeds, doing wonders?
>
> (Exodus 15:11 ESV)
>
> Let all the earth fear the Lord; let all the inhabitants of the world stand in awe of him!
>
> (Psalm 33:8 NKJV)

6. **Putting God upon the throne of our hearts**

> Yours, O Lord, is the greatness, The power and the glory, The victory and the majesty; For all that is in heaven and in earth is Yours; Yours is the kingdom, O Lord, And You are exalted as head over all.
>
> (1 Chronicles 29:11 NKJV)
>
> In the year that King Uzziah died, I saw the Lord sitting on a throne, high and lifted up, and the train of His robe filled the temple. Above it stood seraphim; each one had six wings: with two he covered his face, with two he covered his feet, and with two he flew. And one cried to another and said: "Holy, holy, holy is the Lord of hosts; The whole earth is full of His glory!
>
> (Isaiah 6:1–3 NKJV)

7. **Thinking of God in the fullness of His attributes and character, nothing less**

God's infinitude, immensity, immutability, goodness, justice and wrath, mercy, grace, omnipotence, omniscience, omnipresence, holiness, perfection, self-existence, transcendence, eternalness, sovereignty, wisdom, faithfulness, forgiveness, truth, righteousness, forgiveness, beauty, majesty, and love.

Chapter 35

A Biblical Consideration of God's Perfect Attributes

For those who call themselves Christians, a child of God through Christ Jesus, there is nothing more harmful within their relationship with God than to have developed a pick-and-choose mentality of God's essence. God's nature, His perfection of combined attributes are all-inclusive of who He is in totality, the only true God, "I Am."

To focus solely on certain aspects of God's character and attributes, while trying to negate or forget His other attributes, essentially is to rob Him of His perfect holy nature and His worthiness. This type of imagery of God has not only brought God down to man's level, but it has stripped Him of His perfectness, holiness, and righteousness in our knowledge of Him.

We don't have the right to choose and create a mental image of God to our own liking. We can't afford to be lethargic in our study of our Lord God! For those who can read and have a Bible in their native tongue, claiming ignorance is a feeble excuse, and to ignore God's perfect holiness is contemptible.

Many of today's Christian congregations have created their God whom they worship, rather than worshipping the God of the Bible. Through negligence of sound biblical teaching, scores of believers now view God less than He is in His total perfection, excellence, completeness, and holiness. The result is nothing less than idolatry in worshipping a man-made created God different from what God revealed to us about Himself through His Son, Christ Jesus, the prophets, apostles, and written Word.

One of the most inspiring statements I found most fitting to this topic comes from an excerpt of a sermon given by Charles Spurgeon during his pastorate at Park Street Chapel in London, England. And the words he spoke in 1855 from that pulpit still ring forth with great truth today.

> It has been said by someone that, "the proper study of mankind is man." I will not oppose the idea, but I believe it is equally true that the proper study of God's elect is God; the proper study of a Christian is the Godhead. The highest science, the loftiest speculation, the mightiest philosophy, which can ever engage the attention of a child of God, is the name, the nature, the person, the work, the doings, and the existence of the great God whom he calls his Father. There is something exceedingly improving to the mind in a contemplation of the Divinity. It is a subject so vast, that all our thoughts are lost in its immensity; so deep, that our pride is drowned in its infinity.[39]

---

[39] C. H. Spurgeon archives. http://www.spurgeon.org/sermons/0001.

The evangelical church today has never been in greater need of elevating our knowledge of God through whole biblical truth and nothing less. Bringing God down to our level, to our terms, will never, ever bring glory to God. Let's make no mistake about it! God's majesty and holiness are not to be trifled with, minimized, or marginalized! The depths from which we worship God must come from the truth about God. False pretenses or ideologies about God will only result in false worship of God.

> When the Spirit of truth comes, he will guide you into all the truth, for he will not speak on his own authority, but whatever he hears he will speak, and he will declare to you the things that are to come. He will glorify me, for he will take what is mine and declare it to you.
>
> (John 16:13–14 ESV)
>
> For although they knew God, they did not honor him as God or give thanks to him, but they became futile in their thinking, and their foolish hearts were darkened.
>
> (Romans 1:21 ESV)

I repeat: Let's make no mistake about it! God's majesty and holiness is not to be trifled with, minimized, or marginalized!

Chapter 36

God's Attributes: A Concise Biblical Study

No doubt, we could amass a nearly inexhaustible list depicting the character of God. Having an intimate relationship with Him will often provide tremendous times of reflection and depths of insight, as to God's self-revealing to His children. During my course of studies, I've come to discover that many respected Bible scholars vary in their opinions and commentary of God's character and perfect attributes in their totality of number.

Many books have been written providing significant exposition and reflective discourse regarding the attributes and character of God. Therefore, my purpose is not to attempt to create a comprehensive list for you to study. Rather, my intention is to engage your thoughts in the core essence of who God is, and the fact that there is much more to God than most of us give proper time to think about and to worship.

God's Infinitude

> Great is the Lord! He is most worthy of praise! No one can measure his greatness.
>
> (Psalm 145:3 NLT)

> He counts the stars and calls them all by name.
>
> (Psalm 147:4 NLT)

God's Immensity

> Who else has held the oceans in his hand? Who has measured off the heavens with his fingers? Who else knows the weight of the earth or has weighed the mountains and hills on a scale? Who is able to advise the Spirit of the Lord? Who knows enough to give him advice or teach him? Has the Lord ever needed anyone's advice? Does he need instruction about what is good? Did someone teach him what is right or show him the path of justice? No, for all the nations of the world are but a drop in the bucket. They are nothing more than dust on the scales. He picks up the whole earth as though it were a grain of sand.
>
> (Isaiah 40:12–15 NLT)

God's Immutability

> I am the Lord, and I do not change.
>
> (Malachi 3:6 NLT)

> God also bound himself with an oath, so that those who received the promise could be perfectly sure that he would never change his mind. So God has

given both his promise and his oath. These two things are unchangeable because it is impossible for God to lie.

(Hebrews 6:17–18 NLT)

Whatever is good and perfect comes down to us from God our Father, who created all the lights in the heavens. He never changes or casts a shifting shadow.

(James 1:17 NLT)

God's Goodness

I will tell of the Lord's unfailing love. I will praise the Lord for all he has done. I will rejoice in his great goodness to Israel, which he has granted according to his mercy and love.

(Isaiah 63:7 NLT)

Now all glory to God, who is able to keep you from falling away and will bring you with great joy into his glorious presence without a single fault.

(Jude 24 NLT)

God's Justice and Wrath

For the Lord your God is the God of gods and Lord of lords. He is the great God, the mighty and awesome God, who shows no partiality and cannot be bribed.

(Deuteronomy 10:17 NLT)

Dark clouds surround him. Righteousness and justice are the foundation of his throne.

(Psalm 97:2 NLT)

God's Mercy

But the mercy of the Lord is from everlasting to everlasting On those who fear Him, And His righteousness to children's children.

(Psalm 103:17 NKJV)

All praise to God, the Father of our Lord Jesus Christ. God is our merciful Father and the source of all comfort.

(2 Corinthians 1:3 NLT)

The faithful love of the Lord never ends! His mercies never cease.

(Lamentations 3:22 NLT)

God's Grace

From his abundance we have all received one gracious blessing after another. For the law was given through Moses, but God's unfailing love and faithfulness came through Jesus Christ.

(John 1:16–17 NLT)

Yet God, with undeserved kindness, declares that we are righteous. He did this through Christ Jesus when he freed us from the penalty for our sins.

(Romans 3:24 NLT)

God's Omnipotence

> Jesus looked at them intently and said, "Humanly speaking, it is impossible. But with God everything is possible."
>
> (Matthew 19:26 NLT)

> For nothing is impossible with God.
>
> (Luke 1:37 NLT)

> And I heard, as it were, the voice of a great multitude, as the sound of many waters and as the sound of mighty thunderings, saying, "Alleluia! For the Lord God Omnipotent reigns!"
>
> (Revelation 19:6 NKJV)

God's Omnipresence

> But will God really live on earth? Why, even the highest heavens cannot contain you. How much less this Temple I have built!
>
> (1 Kings 8:27 NLT)

> I can never escape from your Spirit! I can never get away from your presence! If I go up to heaven, you are there; if I go down to the grave, you are there. If I ride the wings of the morning, if I dwell by the farthest oceans, even there your hand will guide me, and your strength will support me.
>
> (Psalm 139:7–10 NLT)

God's Omniscience

> Oh, how great are God's riches and wisdom and knowledge! How impossible it is for us to understand his decisions and his ways! For who can know the Lord's thoughts? Who knows enough to give him advice? And who has given him so much that he needs to pay it back? For everything comes from him and exists by his power and is intended for his glory. All glory to him forever! Amen.

> (Romans 11:33–36 NLT)

> How great is our Lord! His power is absolute! His understanding is beyond comprehension!

> (Psalm 147:5 NLT)

God's Holiness

> They were calling out to each other, "Holy, holy, holy is the Lord of Heaven's Armies! The whole earth is filled with his glory!"

> (Isaiah 6:3 NLT)

> Who is like you among the gods, O Lord—glorious in holiness, awesome in splendor, performing great wonders?

> (Exodus 15:11 NLT)

God's Perfection

> "To whom will you compare me? Who is my equal?" asks the Holy One.

> (Isaiah 40:25 NLT)

> But you are to be perfect, even as your Father in heaven is perfect.
>
> (Matthew 5:48 NLT)

God's Self-Existence

> Christ is the visible image of the invisible God. He existed before anything was created and is supreme over all creation, for through him God created everything in the heavenly realms and on earth. He made the things we can see and the things we can't see—such as thrones, kingdoms, rulers, and authorities in the unseen world. Everything was created through him and for him. He existed before anything else, and he holds all creation together.
>
> (Colossians 1:15–17 NLT)

God's Transcendence

> He alone can never die, and he lives in light so brilliant that no human can approach him. No human eye has ever seen him, nor ever will. All honor and power to him forever! Amen.
>
> (1 Timothy 6:16 NLT)

> Yours, O Lord, is the greatness, the power, the glory, the victory, and the majesty. Everything in the heavens and on earth is yours, O Lord, and this is your kingdom. We adore you as the one who is over all things.
>
> (1 Chronicles 29:11 NLT)

God's Eternalness

> Lord, through all the generations you have been our home! Before the mountains were born, before you gave birth to the earth and the world, from beginning to end, you are God.
>
> (Psalm 90:1–2 NLT)
>
> The high and lofty one who lives in eternity, the Holy One, says this: "I live in the high and holy place with those whose spirits are contrite and humble. I restore the crushed spirit of the humble and revive the courage of those with repentant hearts.
>
> (Isaiah 57:15 NLT)

God's Sovereignty

> So remember this and keep it firmly in mind: The Lord is God both in heaven and on earth, and there is no other.
>
> (Deuteronomy 4:39 NLT)
>
> How great are his signs, how powerful his wonders! His kingdom will last forever, his rule through all generations.
>
> (Daniel 4:3 NLT)

God's Wisdom

> But God made the earth by his power, and he preserves it by his wisdom. With his own understanding he stretched out the heavens.
>
> (Jeremiah 10:12 NLT)

God's purpose in all this was to use the church to display his wisdom in its rich variety to all the unseen rulers and authorities in the heavenly places.

(Ephesians 3:10 NLT)

God's Faithfulness

I will sing of the Lord's unfailing love forever! Young and old will hear of your faithfulness. Your unfailing love will last forever. Your faithfulness is as enduring as the heavens.

(Psalm 89:1–2 NLT)

If we are unfaithful, he remains faithful, for he cannot deny who he is.

(2 Timothy 2:13 NLT)

God's Forgiveness

But if we are living in the light, as God is in the light, then we have fellowship with each other, and the blood of Jesus, his Son, cleanses us from all sin.

(1 John 1:7 NLT)

But if we confess our sins to him, he is faithful and just to forgive us our sins and to cleanse us from all wickedness.

(1 John 1:9 NLT)

My dear children, I am writing this to you so that you will not sin. But if anyone does sin, we have an advocate who pleads our case before the Father. He is Jesus Christ, the one who is truly righteous.

(1 John 2:1 NLT)

He has removed our sins as far from us as the east is from the west.

(Psalm 103:12 NLT)

God's Truthfulness

Jesus told him, "I am the way, the truth, and the life. No one can come to the Father except through me."

(John 14:6 NLT)

And we know that the Son of God has come, and he has given us understanding so that we can know the true God. And now we live in fellowship with the true God because we live in fellowship with his Son, Jesus Christ. He is the only true God, and he is eternal life.

(1 John 5:20 NLT)

Then I saw heaven opened, and a white horse was standing there. Its rider was named Faithful and True, for he judges fairly and wages a righteous war.

(Revelation 19:11 NLT)

God's Righteousness

> But the Lord reigns forever, executing judgment from his throne. He will judge the world with justice and rule the nations with fairness.
>
> (Psalm 9:7–8 NLT)

> Righteousness and justice are the foundation of your throne. Unfailing love and truth walk before you as attendants. Happy are those who hear the joyful call to worship, for they will walk in the light of your presence, Lord. They rejoice all day long in your wonderful reputation. They exult in your righteousness.
>
> (Psalm 89:14–16 NLT)

God's Beauty

> From Mount Zion, the perfection of beauty, God shines in glorious radiance.
>
> (Psalm 50:2 NLT)

God's Majesty

> There is no one like the God of Israel. He rides across the heavens to help you, across the skies in majestic splendor.
>
> (Deuteronomy 33:26 NLT)

> The Son radiates God's own glory and expresses the very character of God, and he sustains everything by the mighty power of his command. When he had cleansed us from our sins, he sat down in the

place of honor at the right hand of the majestic God in heaven."

(Hebrews 1:3 NLT)

God's Love

Dear friends, let us continue to love one another, for love comes from God. Anyone who loves is a child of God and knows God. But anyone who does not love does not know God, for God is love. God showed how much he loved us by sending his one and only Son into the world so that we might have eternal life through him. This is real love—not that we loved God, but that he loved us and sent his Son as a sacrifice to take away our sins.

(1 John 4:7–10 NLT)

For God loved the world so much that he gave his one and only Son, so that everyone who believes in him will not perish but have eternal life.

(John 3:16 NLT)

No power in the sky above or in the earth below—indeed, nothing in all creation will ever be able to separate us from the love of God that is revealed in Christ Jesus our Lord.

(Romans 8:39 NLT)

Holy, Holy, Holy

Holy, holy, holy! Lord God Almighty!
Early in the morning our song shall rise to Thee;
Holy, holy, holy, merciful and mighty!
God in three Persons, blessed Trinity!

Holy, holy, holy! All the saints adore Thee,
Casting down their golden crowns around the glassy sea;
Cherubim and seraphim falling down before Thee,
Who was, and is, and evermore shall be.

Holy, holy, holy! though the darkness hide Thee,
Though the eye of sinful man Thy glory may not see;
Only Thou art holy; there is none beside Thee,
Perfect in power, in love, and purity.

Holy, holy, holy! Lord God Almighty!
All Thy works shall praise Thy name, in earth, and sky, and sea;
Holy, holy, holy; merciful and mighty!
God in three Persons, blessed Trinity![40]

---

40 "Holy, Holy, Holy," lyrics by Reginald Heber (1826).

Prayerful Closing

I pray for the body of believers, for those who call upon the Lord as their Savior, to humbly beseech the mercies of His grace until we behold the majesty of His glory. With wholehearted sincerity, let us seek the fullness of God with all diligence and impassioned desire that we would trust in Him with full certainty, as He is faithful to hear our prayers and delights in the truth uttered from the hearts of His children.

Through the wisdom of God the Father, the goodness and grace of Christ Jesus, and the power of the Holy Spirit, all things can be transformed for the glory of God and for our good. For we are the manifold joys of Christ, His bride, seen throughout all heaven as radiant and pure. May we realize that one day we will become that which was ordained by God from without beginning and will remain forever without end, through Christ's future glorious appearing!

Though we seemingly are surrounded by a number of barriers, we must take courage and realize, that no plan of God's that was designed before time began will ever fall short of His perfect ultimate purpose. Nothing He has ordered to come to fruition will ever fail or come short of the mark. Let us take comfort in knowing, that nothing within the church occurs by happenstance or apart from His knowledge or sovereign control. Ever watching, protecting, guiding, and loving, God remains faithful even when we are not.

Let us confess to God of the barriers we've allowed to be established in our own lives and corporately within our times of gathering. Let each of us resolve to ask God for the wisdom and strength to remove the rubble and stumbling blocks, preventing us from revival. May we come together in unity, seeking to be restored to the manifest presence of God and with a great fervent desire to forgo our many accustomed entertainments and to pursue only that which is holy, pleasing and acceptable unto God - Amen!

Timothy's Mission

All proceeds from sales of this book will be used to further the gospel and build up the body of Christ. With both focused purpose and tremendous passion, it is my earnest commitment to further preach the gospel and share my testimony of God's faithfulness. In the event you would like to purchase additional copies of this book, you can do so online through Family Discipleship Ministries (familydiscipleshipministries.org), or at online retail booksellers.

For correspondence and booking:
timmauricio7@gmail.com
www.timothysmission.org